T0062521

START SCREAMING MURDER

Talmage Powell

Adams Media
New York London Toronto Sydney New Delhi

Adams Media
An Imprint of Simon & Schuster, Inc.
57 Littlefield Street
Avon, Massachusetts 02322

Copyright © 1962 by Talmage Powell.

All rights reserved, including the right to reproduce this book or portions thereof
in any form whatsoever. For information address Adams Media Subsidiary Rights
Department, 1230 Avenue of the Americas, New York, NY 10020.

ADAMS MEDIA and colophon are trademarks of Simon & Schuster, Inc.

For information about special discounts for bulk purchases, please
contact Simon & Schuster Special Sales at 1-866-506-1949 or business@
simonandschuster.com.

Manufactured in the United States of America

Library of Congress Cataloging-in-Publication Data has been applied for.

ISBN 978-1-4405-5598-5
ISBN 978-1-4405-3694-6 (ebook)

This is a work of fiction. Names, characters, corporations, institutions,
organizations, events, or locales in this novel are either the product of the
author's imagination or, if real, used fictitiously. The resemblance of any
character to actual persons (living or dead) is entirely coincidental.

This work has been previously published in print format by:
Pocket Books of Canada, Ltd.

Start Screaming Murder

Chapter One

She was hiding in my apartment when I got back there that night. She didn't use the windows or doors. She had her own way of getting in—and her own brand of trouble.

The evening had started with a minor annoyance. At 10:03 a burglar alarm went off in a Franklin Street jewelry store. Four cops, courtesy the city of Tampa, Florida, checked the corners and cracks and found nobody in the place.

I was called because I'm the agent in charge of the southeastern office of Nationwide Detective Agency. Part of our bread comes from installing and servicing burglar alarms.

The system was independent of city electricity, operating on a six-cell, series-wired dry pack. A defect in one of the cells had gummed up the works. I'd brought my kit along. I replaced the cell, chinned briefly with the city cops, pushed my way through the rubber-neckers on the sidewalk, and headed for home.

I was hot, tired and thirsty as I ran the car into the long, ramshackle shed behind the beatup apartment building on the edge of Ybor City, Tampa's old-worldish Latin quarter.

I started down the scabby, brick side of the building. I didn't know he was there until he brought the sap down right where my brown mat is thinning on the crown of my head.

Six feet, a hundred and ninety pounds, and forty-odd years of Ed Rivers pitched face foremost on the dirty crushed shell of the alley.

The loose-shell paving ground my cheek. I fought off un-

1

consciousness, snarling for breath. I heard him breathing, quick and hard. His hands pummeled my body, trying to find my pockets. He passed up the wallet. When my keys rattled, his hand quickened.

The first spectacular burst of fireworks cleared out of my head. I reared around and shot the heel of my shoe straight at his groin. It connected, like my shoe had connected with tough, tight-stretched cowhide.

He grunted softly and rocked back. The sap came whistling at me again.

His first blow had been without personal feeling. He was sore now. The purpose of the blackjack was to lay my brains in the alley like scrambled eggs in a steaming pan.

I pitched to one side. The plaited leather over the coil spring handle of the sap nipped my ear. The weapon slapped across my shoulder. My left arm went numb, as if it had been detached from me.

I got a quick impression of a guy who topped me by four inches and twenty-five pounds. Wearing greasy ducks, T-shirt, and a dirty yachting cap, he was solid as a prairie steer.

I saw the glint of his teeth, the redness of his eyes. He was swinging the sap again, a short curse in his mouth. I went in under the blackjack. When I felt him slam against the building I knew my numb shoulder had connected. His curse was smothered by the air tearing out of him.

His first deadly speed was braked a little. He grabbed for my throat with his left hand, trying to get my head in sapping position. I hit him in the face with my right hand, heard the back of his head hit the brick. His knees caved for a second.

If he hadn't had the advantage of that first dirty blow, I'd have got him right then. He knew it. As I went in, he lost his head and began swinging the sap wildly, lashing me across the back and buttocks.

Grogginess had my timing off. The sap was plenty rough. I had to get away from the punishment pouring across my ribs.

I rolled back, and he thought he had me. In the wan light

filtering from the street, I saw his face. His lips and chin were wet with spit. The red hunger in his eyes was like a flame.

I let the eagerness of the blackjack bring him nice and close. Just as the sap poised, I brought my right fist straight in from center field. For an instant, he didn't have a nose, just a big, flat, bloody mess for a face. He bounced like a crazy cue ball in a bank shot. He did a cross between a jitterbug step and Virginia reel, halfway across the alley.

Most men would have gone down and stayed for awhile. This guy didn't. He caromed off the building and started out of the alley. He moved like a drunk who wakes up to find the building on fire.

He turned the bloody moon of face toward me, throwing quick glances. Every time I stretched my legs, his stretched a little further. As he rounded the corner, he was gaining momentum with every slap of his feet.

I slowed down, staggered to a halt. Sucking at air, my mouth open, I knew I couldn't catch him. Right then, it wouldn't have been smart to start searching for him. There were too many other alleys and dark places—for me to try with one arm and half my senses.

I put my hand against the building to keep the world from rocking too much. Reaction hit the bottom of my stomach. I stood swaying, waiting for the sickness to pass.

My left arm started welding itself back to my body, an operation without benefit of pain killer. Sweat broke on my face. I gathered up the left forearm with my right and hugged it to me.

This time I got sick for real.

Five or six minutes later, I hauled myself inside the building. The heat, musty age, and lingering spice of Cuban cooking closed over me. The building had taken no notice of what had happened in the alley. There was an old, quiet creaking tiredness in the swayed floors and walls and ceiling. The gloom was almost inaudibly accented by the sorrowful, muffled whisper of a Spanish guitar in the bowels of the building. The guitar murmured of a man alone in half-darkness with yearnings peculiar to the Latin heart.

A dim bulb was burning in the second floor hall. I saw that the ancient wicker hall table had been pushed close to my door.

I didn't think anything of the table being there. It roamed the building, as tenants had guests for cards, dominoes, or *arroz con pollo*.

I fished out my keys and gave them a look. The punk had seemed to want those keys. In fact, he'd been desperate enough to try to sap me to get the keys.

I couldn't figure it. There was nothing in the apartment worth stealing. If he was after something out of my office in downtown Tampa, it would have been a lot more sensible for him to break in.

I keyed the apartment door open, stepped inside, and turned on a lamp. The apartment was a lot like my office. Not much. There was a daybed for sweat-washed sleep, a TV I didn't watch often, a kitchenette, a huge old bathroom with gargling plumbing.

I made for the bathroom first. I ran the water until it was cooler than tepid, soaked my head, and washed the grit off my face.

In the medicine-cabinet mirror, the face stared back at me, heavy, bearish, dark-tanned and creased, the thick lids giving the brown eyes a lazy look. Women either get a charge from the face or want to run from it. Men fear it, or trust it to the hilt. It isn't a face that ever meets a neutral reaction. I'm not always happy about that, but it's my face and I have to do the best I can with it.

Right now, I was interested in the damage done to the face. It could have been worse. The bits of crushed shell had hamburgered the skin on my cheek, but the skin on my head hadn't been broken.

I started cold water into the bathtub. While it was running,

I soaked a wash cloth and laid it gingerly on the tender swelling on my skull.

Continually working my left arm and shoulder against the subsiding pain and creeping stiffness, I headed toward the kitchen where cold beer waited in the refrigerator.

I opened the refrigerator door—and right then, I wasn't alone again. I knew it, with that quick tightening around the heart, the squeezed-up feeling at the nape of the neck.

I pitched my head compress into the sink, dropped in a crouch as I spun toward the sibilant softness of another person's breathing.

For a second, I thought I must be hearing things. There wasn't another soul in the kitchenette with me.

Then she came walking from the cave of shadows underneath the kitchenette table.

"Ed . . ." she said. "Take it easy! It's me—Tina La Flor."

I wiped my sleeve across my forehead and stared at Tina the Flower.

When I say she was a living doll, I mean it literally. She had a calendar-girl figure, sunny-reddish hair that rippled to her shoulders, green eyes with a tiny up-tilt at the corners, and a face so mistily beautiful that you had to look twice at the porcelain perfection of it to make sure it was real.

And after that second look, along about the third or fourth look, you felt your heart break a little on her account. Because all that perfectly proportioned, out-of-this-world loveliness was a sleek package that stood slightly over three feet high when she cleared the table top and straightened up.

In a doll-sized black dress, nylons sheer as baby cobwebs, and tiny black shoes with spike heels like toothpicks, she lifted a perfect pink hand, no bigger than two of my fingers, and pointed at my face.

"You . . . run into a door, Ed?"

"Yeah, with two arms and legs and a head full of intentions right out of a sewer."

She paled slightly, avoided my eyes, and walked into the

bed-sittingroom. Watching her made me think of the chick of a slick magazine illustration seen through the wrong end of a telescope.

She came to an indecisive halt in the middle of the room. A shiver crossed her shoulders. With her back toward me, she asked faintly, "You got a drink, Ed?"

"Beer's all."

The spun copper of her hair washed across her shoulders as she shook her head. "That stuff's too puny. Anyhow, I need to watch my figure."

"I'll order a jug from the package store."

"No, I really don't need the drink."

"I'll be glad to . . ."

"I know. But I wouldn't take a drink now if I had it. For a second there. . . . Why don't you go ahead and have your beer?"

While I opened and poured beer, I thought of the attack in the alley and Tina's presence here. I began to explore the realm of ideas.

Studying her out of the corner of my eyes, I wondered what kind of trouble she was in. There are a lot of midgets in this country, so many of the proud, smart Little People that they hold periodic national conventions and elect their own president.

Tampa developed into a kind of home base for many of them years ago when the carnivals began winter-quartering in the area. The Little People are mainly big citizens. Few of them get into trouble, but I suspected I knew one who had a bigger package of woe on her tiny shoulders than most of us normal-sized human beings are ever faced with.

I carried the beer into the bed-sittingroom. Tina had perched on the end of the couch. I hadn't seen her in several months. I'd got to know her pretty well when she headlined the show at the Latin Club. They'd billed her as the "World's Tiniest and Most Beautiful Chanteuse," which was a pleasant and fairly accurate honesty. I don't go in much for nightclubbing, but the Latin, under the old management had the best food and draft in town, which attracted some interesting conversationalists.

I stood in front of Tina and looked meaningfully from her to the open transom over my door. "It's a wonder," I said, "that you didn't break a leg, climbing that old wicker hall table, shinnying over the transom and dropping inside the apartment. He sure must have been hot on your heels."

"He was, Ed," she said, like she'd tasted a bitter green apple.

"So he couldn't get in without rousing the whole house, and you didn't dare go back out where there wouldn't be a locked door between you."

"Something like that," she said in a small voice.

"And then he lays for me—to get a key to this door."

She bit her lips. "I swear, Ed, I thought he'd go away. I didn't know he'd try to knock your brains out."

"Why'd you pick on me, Tina?".

"I was coming to see you. You're a private cop. You work for hire. I needed to hire. Simple enough?"

"So far," I said. "Where does the man figure?"

"He was the job."

I pulled up a chair and took a sip of the beer. "I don't see how we could be talking about different guys, but let's make sure. He was a big fellow, wearing greasy ducks, old yachting cap. Looks like a carny or a seaman on a freighter steaming out of Port Tampa."

"That's him," she said. The shudder touched her again.

"Who is he?"

"Bucks Jordan. I used to know him on a carny circuit. He ran a kewpie-doll concession."

"What'd you do to him?"

"Nothing, Ed. I swear it."

"Then why is he after you?"

A brittle hardness came to her green eyes. "Geez! You ain't a rube. You wasn't born yesterday!"

No, but my mind wouldn't grasp it that quickly. "A masher?"

"You said it."

I nearly dropped the beer. "Tina, a full grown man and a little doll like you. . . ." I didn't mean to say it. Maybe it was in my face without my saying it.

She pressed back against the daybed bolster. A poisonous change took place inside of her, born of a knowledge she carried night and day through all her years. She reminded me of a cornered kitten, back arched and ready to start spitting against torture.

"Tina," I said, "I didn't mean . . ."

"The hell you didn't!" she said in a hoarse whisper. "Maybe you didn't want to mean it, but you couldn't help yourself. You stinking, lousy race of giants! You big hogs staring at the little freak. . . ."

Her breaking voice quit on her. Tears in her eyes, she sat with her hands balled into tiny fists as if she wanted to slug the world of normal-sized tables and chairs and lunch counters and stair steps and wash basins and telephone booths.

I sensed the ghosts in the room right then. The big fat business man getting a laugh out of his pals: "Baby, why don't I put you in my briefcase and sneak you down to the office; my wife would never know." The simpering matron: "My, isn't she the perfect little thing!" The child, around a mouthful of carny cotton candy: "Look, mama, she's no bigger than my dolly. I wish my dolly could sing and dance."

Few were intentionally vicious or cruel. They stared, and they were reassured. They were Big People, and their bigness was added to. And they didn't stop to think that her feelings and emotions were as big as their own.

Chapter Two

I killed the beer and said bluntly, "Okay, so I made a booboo. Like you say, Tina, it wasn't intentional. Blame it on my being human. Now, we going to think about it all night—or this problem of Bucks Jordan?"

She remained a long way off for another moment. Gradually, she came back, wiped her lower lids with a pink-nailed fingertip, and said, "Is that supposed to be an apology?"

"Yes."

A hint of a smile touched her lips. "For a guy as tough as an old bull-elephant, you got a mushpot for a heart, Ed."

"I'm interested in this guy with the free swinging black-jack," I said, "and the reason you headed for me instead of the cops."

"I want the police kept out of it."

"I'll repeat—why?"

"I don't want any publicity. Not that kind."

"Why?"

"Is that all you can say?"

"I'm fishing for your story. You're not making it easy, but you'd better make it good."

She scooted off the daybed and walked to the table where a pack of cigarettes lay on scattered magazines. The fags were beyond her reach. I got up, handed them to her, and struck a paper match for her. The smoke was regular size, no filter, but in her lips it looked like a kingsize.

"Thanks, Ed." She treated herself to several deep, satisfying drags. "Come to think of it, the story may not be so good."

"No?"

"Because it's the truth. The truth does sound lame sometimes, you know."

"I know."

"Maybe I should have made something up," she said, going toward the daybed. She gave me a twisted smile. "But you'd get to the bottom of anything that was made up."

"Let's let the lame truth limp a little," I suggested.

She was calmer now, in no hurry. She stretched, seeming to enjoy the feeling of security the apartment and my presence gave her.

"To begin with," she said, "Bucks Jordan used to be a minor annoyance in my carny days. It was nothing new. You'd be surprised how many guys have made gaga eyes at me."

Knowing something of people, I wasn't very surprised.

"Back then," Tina went on, "Bucks didn't dare cross the line. He had to content himself with colored remarks and a pat on my shoulder when he thought he could get away with it. There were always other people around. The roustabouts worshipped me and would have broken his neck at a snap of my fingers. I was the star of the show, and you know how class-ridden carny and circus society is. Bucks lived in one social stratum, I in another. I avoided him and managed to get through the season without trouble."

Thinking about it, she tensed up and sought relief in the cigarette. With a big cloud of billowing smoke adding to the misty quality of her face, she said, "I didn't think I'd ever see Bucks again. And I didn't, for a long time. Then the other day I bumped into him, in a Tampa restaurant. Since then . . ." She spread her arms. "Ed, I swear I don't think the guy's got all his marbles. He can't get it through his head that I'm not really gone on him."

"Sounds like a creep of the first water."

"You can say that again! Calling me, following me, trying to make dates . . . ugh. . . ." She made a face. "I told him I was going to sic the cops on him. That scared him off for a while. Then, as time passed and he realized I hadn't hollered for the bulls, he got the big-headed idea it was because I was playing hard to get—but not too hard, not that hard. So the threat backfired on me."

"Are we up to tonight?"

"I guess we are," she said. "I've a cottage here, a home roost. My phone rang. It was Bucks, pretty cocky because I hadn't yelled cop. He was coming out to see me. I knew, then, that I needed some help. I told him to lay off or a tough guy named Ed Rivers would tear his arm off and feed it to him for breakfast."

"You were taking a lot on yourself!"

"Don't get sore, Ed. I've got dough. I decided right then to hire you."

"It isn't always that simple and easy, sweetheart. Sometimes I'm busy on another case. And there are jobs I just don't go for."

She spread her arms. "I had to tell him something, didn't I?"

I growled, "Go on."

"Well, I came here. The creep followed me. I was waiting for you outside your door when I heard his voice downstairs. He was asking somebody which apartment was yours. I had to get away from him. That table was handy in the hall . . . Your transom was open . . . and there was Bucks, coming up the stairs."

She stopped speaking and sat looking at me with a helpless, bland innocence I'd never before run into.

In the silence I heard water running. I got up, cut to the bathroom, and turned off the faucet just before the tub spilled over. I pulled the plug and went slowly back to Tina.

She gave me a cherubic smile.

I returned it, only on me the smile wasn't so angelic. "We return to the groove in the broken record. Why?"

"Ed . . ."

"Cops," I said. "Why me instead of cops?"

"I've explained . . ."

"No, you haven't. You've said you didn't want publicity."

"Isn't that understandable?"

"To an extent. But under the circumstances . . ."

"Okay," she said. "I'll spell it out. I got a new manager. He's in New York right now, and things are really looking great. A month from now I hope to be auditioning for the right people, the really big people. I've got a new routine. It's great, Ed. I know it'll sell me to top clubs, maybe even spots on network variety TV. But to sell I've got to be everything sweet, unsullied and wonderful, the way folks want a dainty little creature like me to be.

"Now . . . I scream police and the reporters, even the ones with colds in their heads, smell a story. You get their angle? Little doll and big bohunk.

"You've dealt with the press yourself, Ed. Most of the ink and paper boys are decent citizens. But there are plenty who'd force their crippled grandmothers to do a fan dance if it meant a story.

"They'd dig up everything possible, make it look as if Bucks and I traveled the carny circuits together. And those magazines . . ." She rolled her eyes. "The ones half the people in show business are suing. Can't you just see some of the lurid streamers across their covers? Such as, 'Why Miniature Carny Delilah Gave Her Six-Foot Samson the Air.' "

Tina practically gagged on the cigarette. "Ed, things being as they are, don't even mention cops to me. This has got to be handled quietly, efficiently, and you're the only guy I'd trust with it."

I knuckled the stubble along my jaw. "Tina, coming from anybody else, I don't know. I'd wonder if it was a lot of cock-and-bull, if you'd told me everything."

"Well, I warned you that the truth . . ."

"It's screwy enough to be true," I admitted. "What, exactly, do you want me to do?"

"Do?" she yelled with a temperamental outsweeping of her arms. "Do what any red-blooded guy your size and weight would do. Look up Bucks and tell him you'll break his stinking neck if he so much as lets my name slip into his foul mind."

"You think it'll work?"

"I know it will. He's a rotten coward. I saw the way he kept his distance when those carny roustabouts were around. He laid off while he thought a big cop was warned and waiting, didn't he? And I'll bet he opened all jets to get away from you in the alley."

"He was plenty mean and tough for a while."

"Yeah? I know what I'm talking about. You put the fear of Ed Rivers in him and he'll sulk about it and find some other doll to pester. I hope to hell she stands five-feet-eight and wrestled under the name of Madame Frankenstein."

She gave me a child-like look of trust which began to glimmer out. "You—you'll do it, Ed?"

"My instincts are cautious," I said.

"What's that mean? You're not afraid of Bucks Jordan. That couldn't be!"

"I got a healthy respect for his size," I said.

"But he tried to break your head! You wouldn't let him, or anybody else in this town, get away with that!"

"Not happily."

"Then what's the hurdle?"

"Sure you've included all the details?"

"Cross my heart." She crossed her heart.

She waited—then she bounced angrily off the daybed and headed for another cigarette.

When I moved toward the table to help her, she snapped, "Never mind!" She stood on tiptoe, strained, and reached the smokes and matches. "I'm used to helping myself in this outsized world you big gorillas have created for yourselves. I guess I can keep right on." She ignored the match I offered and struck one of her own.

Crossing the room swiftly, she posed martyr-like at the door. "I'll try to feel no rancor, Ed. Please give me a little sorrow if you read in the papers that I've been criminally assaulted and . . ."

"Oh, shut up," I said.

She came to center-stage with perfect timing, real tears of gratitude sparkling in her eyes. "Does this mean . . ."

"Where do I find Bucks Jordan?"

"Darling!" she screamed daintily. "I knew you would . . ."

"Pipe down and take it easy," I said. "Like you say, Nationwide is in business for a purpose. We are for hire, and I'd like to feed Bucks the handle off his blackjack for personal reasons."

"He's been working on a boat, Ed. A private job. A big schooner, the kind capable of a South Seas trip. It's called the *Sprite.*"

"Who owns it?"

"A fellow named Lessard, Alex Lessard, and his daughter. She's called D. D."

"I take it that the *Sprite* is at anchorage in this area?"

"Right in Tampa Bay."

"This will cost you the going rate of seventy-five bucks a day and expenses."

"Sounds like a bargain."

"You'll have to sign contracts. We'll meet at my office early and . . ."

"Meet my eye! I'm staying right here, Ed, until you put some nails in Bucks Jordan's hide. You just park the cushions off that old club chair in the kitchen—any corner will do—and give me a blanket. I won't be any bother and very little expense. I have half an egg for breakfast."

Chapter Three

Tina's inherent romanticism had visualized the *Sprite* with her bow cutting through a South Sea, the Pacific swishing past with a sound like rustling hula skirts.

Which goes to show you.

A couple hundred yards off-shore, the *Sprite* was a mean old tiger taken with a case of mange. There was nothing jaunty in the solid set of the schooner's two masts against the brazen sky. Crouched in the oily, dead heat, she was dirty and needed paint. A rich man looking for a toy would have passed her over. A knowledgeable sailor looking for guts in a craft might have picked her up for a tenth of her actual worth.

I was driving a shiny new sedan, purchased with agency funds, a departure from our previous practice of annual leasing from an auto rental outfit.

I drove the car down the short asphalt road to a scabby bait camp. A couple of lean guys in jeans were tinkering with an outboard motor on a bench set up beneath towering pines.

One of them came toward me when I got out of the car. Wiping his hands on a piece of waste, he said howdy.

"I'd like to get out to the *Sprite*," I said. "That's her, isn't it?"

"Yep. Rent you a flat-bottom." He preceded me to the weathered wooden pier where water lapped against a dozen or more skiffs, each tied in its slip.

In his thirties, burned leather-brown by the sun, the proprietor moved with the resilience of bamboo.

15

"I'm looking for a fellow I know," I said. "Works on the *Sprite*. His name is Bucks Jordan."

"Then row out and see him."

"I thought you might . . ."

"Look, Mister. I don't know anything about that boat or the people on her. You want the flat-bottom?"

"I don't feel like swimming."

"It'll be two dollars."

Rowing out to the schooner, I was miserable in the heat. Sweat poured off me, plastering clothes and sodden flesh together in a stifling mess. The heat became a pulse beat in my head and solar plexus. I've been down here nearly twenty years, and I've never got used to the heat.

Sometimes I almost ache for a frosty New Jersey morning. I've never gone back, not since I was a young beat cop up there. Maybe there are too many memories. Of a girl I knew once. She ran away with a punk I was trying to nail. Their fast moving car met an equally fast freight at a crossing.

I blotted out the next few years with alcohol. One morning I woke in an alley, in the crummiest part of Ybor City. I knew it was dry out or die. I took a job on the docks and dried out. Later, Nationwide gave me a break, a job. As the years passed, Tampa became my home. At times I felt as if I'd been born here.

The mangrove-tangled shoreline fell behind. Far off to my port stern, the buildings of downtown Tampa showed rectangular silhouettes in the shimmering pall of heat that was the sky.

As I neared the schooner, a red-hot cruiser roared past fanning a wake that almost capsized the flat-bottom. I grabbed the ladder of the *Sprite* and held on until the flat-bottom relaxed.

When I looked up, I saw a woman on the schooner's deck. She was watching me silently. She was, I guessed, in her early twenties. You think of many females that age as "girls." This one you didn't. She was short, heavy-breasted, full-faced.

Almost stocky. Her hair was a light, faded-looking brown, braided and coiled about her head. She was one of those who come from girlhood into womanhood, by-passing the adolescent phase. She would pass for a very competent secretary, a person capable of assuming responsibilities beyond the scope of a mere girl.

"Hello," I said.

"Who are you?"

"The name is Ed Rivers."

"What do you want?"

"I'm looking for Mr. Lessard. Are you his daughter, D. D.?"

"No. I'm Maria Scanlon, a friend of the Lessards. . . . If you're coming aboard, you'd better snub the line or you'll lose the flat-bottom."

I snubbed the line and climbed on deck. "Is Mr. Lessard here?"

"Below. He'll be up in a minute." She motioned with a square, graceless hand toward a decrepit deck chair. I went over and sat down. Like everything else about the *Sprite* the chair was a lot stronger, more sinewy than it appeared. I took out my handkerchief and started wiping some of the steam off my face.

"You're not a very good sailor, Mr. Rivers," she said, with a laugh. The laugh did things for her, wiping away some of the seriousness and intensity that was almost middle-age-ish.

"Afraid I'm not," I admitted.

"I watched the way you handled the flat-bottom."

"Do you sail much, Miss Scanlon?"

"Mrs. Scanlon," she corrected. The laugh wasn't even a memory in her face now. "Mr. Rivers," she said quietly, "I believe you are looking for something, listening for a sound. Do you mind my asking what it is?"

I gave her a fresh appraisal. "Is a fellow named Bucks Jordan on board?"

Her eyes held on my face for a second longer. Then she

turned quickly, rounded the cabin, and called, "Alex, there's a man here looking for Jordan."

Quick footsteps. Lessard stood with his hand on the rail, looked me over; the rubber soles of his sneakers cried softly as he came toward the foredeck.

He was a small man, sandy in coloring, maybe forty years old, maybe fifty, or sixty. He had a thin, brooding face, gray eyes like a bitter New England winter. He had lost his hair except for a horseshoe around the sides and back of his long, narrow skull.

In addition to the sneakers, he wore old khaki bathing trunks. He had spindly legs and arms like broom handles. But I didn't let it fool me. The broom handles were overlaid with layers of wires, and the legs had that slightly bowed, knotty quality that you see on a first-rate lightweight boxer. I had the feeling that this guy didn't give much of a damn about anything. It was in his eyes and face. He could take care of himself in the toughest ports in the world—and very probably had—because he wouldn't care whether he lived or died.

Mrs. Maria Scanlon introduced us, and Alex Lessard said, "What you want with Jordan?"

"It's personal."

"Yeah? You a cop?"

"In a way."

"What in hell does that mean? You are, or you aren't."

"A private cop."

"Fancy that. I never saw one of you fellows before. Tell you what. When you locate Bucks Jordan, you let me know and I'll add twenty bucks to whatever you've been paid."

"Then he isn't here?"

"He not only isn't here, Rivers. He took some money with him."

"Wages, Alex," Maria Scanlon said.

"Advance wages," he corrected. "And why don't you stay out of it." He fished cigarettes from the bellyband of the bathing trunks. There were matches pushed under the cellophane covering of the package. He lighted a cigarette and said, "Jordan came aboard to do some work, repairs on the rigging, general cleaning up, painting. He worked for several days. Then he gave me such a wild story about his cracker father being in jail charged with illegal alligator hunting that I handed over a sizable advance."

"You haven't seen Jordan since?"

"No."

"When was this?"

"Couple days ago." Lessard grunted. "The sonofabitch."

"Alex," Maria said, "he's no dog, really. He's a human being, in great part the result of what society. . . ."

"Maria, honey, please. If it hadn't been for your do-gooding talk, I might not have let Jordan. . . ."

"I think you're blaming him prematurely, Alex. He may come back."

Jawing at each other, they'd about forgot I was there. Then Lessard remembered. "How about letting me know if you find him, Rivers?"

"Any idea where he is?"

His face flared with impatience. "If I had, would I be trying to spend twenty bucks with you?"

"I guess not."

"Damn right I wouldn't." He glanced toward the shore. "I wonder what's keeping D. D.?"

"Department store downtown," Maria Scanlon said. "Tell her I had to get back."

"You're going ashore?"

"Yes, if Mr. Rivers will give me a lift."

"Sure," I said.

We clambered into the flat-bottom. She was first, and she picked up the oars. There is only one way to handle the fanatical, smothering type of woman. I took the oars firmly from her, pushed her forward, and started grunting us landward.

"Really, Mr. Rivers, wouldn't it make more sense for the most efficient . . ."

"I'll row, lady," I said.

When we docked the boat, she thanked me and started walking away.

"You live here at the camp?" I nodded toward the cottages drowsing fifty yards away under the tall pines.

"No, down the secondary road a couple of miles."

"I'll drop you off," I said.

"Really, I . . ."

"It's no bother. "I'm going that way."

We got in my sturdy new car and I drove out of the camp and picked up the cracked asphalt.

She sneaked a glance at me. "Why do you want Bucks. . . . But you can't discuss that, can you?"

"Not very well."

"Whatever he's done, are you sure he's to blame?"

I let it ride.

"People are prone to animal-like reactions, you know," she persisted. "Sufficiently goaded, they are liable to snarl back."

"People are also accountable," I reminded her.

"Really?" she said, a disdainful quirk in her heavy brow.

I wondered what her background was. Her diction was good. Her clothes were cheap cotton, but she wore them casually, as if the cost of clothing as she was growing up had never been a major consideration.

I reduced her to little-girl size in my mind, and I had a picture of a kid who was overweight, eager, rebuffed. The one who got her pigtails pulled. The one who never was invited to a prom.

"When did you last see Bucks?" I asked.

"Let's see. . . . Four nights ago, I think it was. He was drinking heavily in a juke joint near here. I got him back to the boat. I can't tell you anything about him, Mr. Rivers. Really. You turn here. There is the cottage."

"If you want to help him," I said, "let me know if you see him."

She wasn't paying attention. She was watching the cottage anxiously.

I thrust one of my cards in her hand. "Call this number. If I'm out, there's a telephone answering service. If I get to Bucks in time, I might be able to save him serious trouble."

She got a focus on the card. "All right," she said. She thrust the card in her dress pocket. Again she looked toward the cottage. It was a cheap, frame affair with a screened porch across the front. A fairly recent model car was parked close to the cottage.

"I suppose Jack's asleep," she mused. "He's my husband. He likes to nap until mid-morning."

Mid-morning was two hours ago. She got out of the car and ran toward the cottage with eagerness. The tall, strapping outlines of a man appeared behind the porch screening; so I guessed Jack wasn't asleep.

The screen door banged behind Maria Scanlon. The man grabbed her arm, jerked her around. He spoke to her, glancing toward the car. Then he shoved her inside, his grip on her arm bringing a small cry from her.

I put the car in gear. Bucks Jordan was my problem. Jack Scanlon was hers.

Chapter Four

It was a long, hot afternoon. I was doing it the hard way, Bucks wasn't in the phone book or city directory. No gas or light bills had been issued to him. Without a lead in those directions, I called on a one-time carny owner I knew and got a list of six names. The third name was a skinny tattoo artist who gave me an address.

The gloomy old house was presided over by a landlady who smelled like soured suet. Bucks no longer lived there. But she told me of a bar where he used to hang out.

At the bar I got a second address, where I picked up the name of another bar. So it goes.

At the bar, it turned out I'd missed Bucks by less than an hour. The bartender said Bucks had been in a real funk, his face showing the results of a clobbering, the inner man seething with the memory of it. He'd been drinking. Not heavily. Just enough to keep a mean edge whetted. He'd made a statement about calling at a doll house.

"Whatever the hell that means," the bartender said with a shrug. I thanked him, and he said, "Any time, Ed."

I began to dig the doll house remark, and I wondered if Bucks was already out there. Thinking about it caused a prickle to chase over my skin.

The cottage was on a street off Nebraska Avenue. It sparkled with a coat of fresh, white paint. A modest frame house with green shutters and high-peaked gables, it was snug behind sheltering hedges and palms.

With my car half a block away, I walked past the cottage. The sun was spewing to a fiery death in the Gulf, with the twilight promising no relief from the heat. Several nearby houses showed lights. This one didn't, but I hadn't expected him to turn on a light, if he was in there.

I did a quick survey. The street was quiet. Ducking down the side yard, I went to the rear door of the cottage. I used the steel on my keyring and was inside in a few seconds. I closed the door gently.

The interior was silent, a vacuum of heat sucking at blood and brains.

In the hot gloom, I experienced the weird feeling of having magically become two or three times my normal size. The furnishings did it. The custom-made kitchen equipment was no higher than eighteen inches. In the dining room, I barked my knee on the corner of the table. It had a matching buffet, china closet, and tiny captain's chairs to match. I couldn't have wedged my bulk on the specially built couch and chairs in the living room. The TV screen looked outsized in a cabinet that snugged it and a hi-fi set close to the luxuriant carpet. The bedroom furniture had been modeled for a fairy princess.

There were low bookcases and tiny tables holding potted greenery, curtains as frothy as sea foam. I was a Gulliver on a modern travel, moving through the world a tiny woman had made for herself. This was Tina La Flor's refuge, her sanctuary.

In the darkening hallway, I wiped my face and considered my next move. My throat was parched. The thought of a cold beer was torture. My guts growled for Cuban sausage and *garbanzo* soup. But my instincts gambled that Bucks Jordan hadn't been here yet. There was no sign of his entry. It was still daylight.

I decided to wait.

In the heat of the closed house, sweat crawled like bugs through the mat on my chest, stained the waistband of my pants, ran down my calves to puddle in my socks.

When it was full dark, he came. I was warned by a scratching on a rear window. I heard a brittle snapping of metal, the sliding of the window. A breath of air slipped into the cottage.

A corner street light was on, and in the murk I saw his shadow creep into the dining room.

He picked up one of the captain's chairs with two fingers, laughed, and threw it on the floor. (With his presence added, the normal-sized house seemed enormous, the tiny furnishings pathetic.)

He padded to the living room. He had a pint bottle in his hip pocket. He pulled it out, slugged it, and recapped it.

He sat down on the carpet, because none of the furniture would hold him, and parked the bottle beside him.

He was facing full toward the entry foyer, and I guessed he was thinking of that moment when she'd step into the room and turn on a light.

"Bucks," I said, "you've made a bad mistake."

I clicked on the dining room light as I spoke. He stopped breathing, literally. For a second he was paralyzed, unable to turn his head. It was exaggerated, like a bit out of an old-time movie that used to bring laughter. But he wasn't comical, not to me. He was the kind who went berserk if he got scared enough. Berserk men can kill, even those a lot smaller than this big slab of beef.

As my shadow belted the waist of the room, he jerked around to a half crouch. His face made me feel a little better about the brawl last night. His nose was a big, purple sausage and there were little yellowish-purple half-moons under each eye.

When he saw who was in the house with him, his eyes went crazy.

His right hand dipped under his shirt and jerked the black-jack from the waistband of his pants.

"You lay off me," he howled. "I ain't scared of you. You lay off . . ."

He made a great try for the foyer. My weight hit him. We

slammed down and a tiny end-table made sounds like crunching eggshells.

My stabbing hand missed, and the sap clipped me on the side of the jaw. I went a little nuts myself, pinned him, and started hitting him in the face. The third or fourth punch caught that swollen nose. A wail came from him. He tore himself free, scrambling toward the dining room. He'd lost the sap. It rolled under my foot, almost pitching me.

I closed on him. He came around swinging the dining-room table. I ducked. The table shattered against the wall.

Before he could regain his balance, I piled into him. His buttocks crashed against the china cabinet and it made glassy tinkling noises.

He was cornered now. He made sledge-hammers of those two big hands and fought back blindly. If he'd held onto his reason, he might have turned the trick. As it was, he was wide open. I hit him until I was sickened, of having to do it, of him making me do it, of myself, because I could think of no other way of controlling him.

Then his knees sagged. He hung as if invisible wires were keeping him from pitching forward. His face was a bloody wreck.

The carpet met his knees. He held to the edge of the buffet to keep from going all the way down.

"Bucks, you're never to bother her again, you understand?"

His head hung forward.

"Be smart and stay healthy," I said. "Don't ever come near Tina La Flor—and I'll forget you exist."

He went crawling toward the living room and the bottle. I wondered if he was crying. The sounds coming from him might have been due to that, or the difficulty he was having in getting air through his blood-clotted throat.

"You got it, Bucks?"

He moaned softly, a sound that shouldn't have belonged to a man. "Please, Rivers . . ."

"You got it?"

"Yeah," he choked. "Only leave me alone. Please leave me alone."

"Just the way you're going to leave the little doll alone. It's a bargain you'd better keep, Bucks."

"Okay," he said. "You know I will." He groped for his bottle.

"Do your drinking some place else, Bucks. She'll be coming back. I'll bring her. She'd better not find you here."

Bowed over, he put his hands over his face and sobbed. "She won't. Only leave me alone, can't you?"

I turned and walked out the back door. My clothes were stuck to me with sweat. But it wasn't the sweat or slight difference in temperature outside that caused me to stop and shudder.

I hurried up the street, got in the car, and U-turned. I hit Nebraska and turned toward Ybor City.

A beer would do. Or a pail of ice water.

I wasn't hungry any longer.

Tina wasn't in the apartment when I got there. She'd left a note: "Ed, I'm gone to eat. Can't take any more of that pepper and hot spice stuff you keep in your refrigerator. What do you use for a stomach, a secondhand bomb casing?"

I grinned at the note and dropped it on the table. Except for breakfast, I didn't eat much in the apartment myself. Tina had been stuck here all day with snack stuff and beer go-withers.

While the tub filled from the cold tap, I stripped down. The final item of apparel was the knife I carry in a sheath at the nape of my neck. It's strictly for those times when all the emergency lights are screaming red. I dislike the knife, but I've owed it my life a few times.

The water temporarily soaked away the heat, along with the tender spots my encounter with Bucks had created.

I was glad it was all over. Tina could go home now and start repairing her lilliputian domain and I could get the bad taste of the whole affair out of my mind.

With fresh clothes on, I felt my appetite returning. It was my turn to leave a note for her: "Stay put until I get back."

It was nice to relax. I ambled a few blocks to a restaurant and, settled for a steak while the tourists at the next table had their first encounter with Spanish squid with rice.

By the time I started back to the apartment, the subtle change of night had come to Ybor City. The Quarter doesn't start jumping in the fully American sense; it slithers; it breathes the air of old Spain and stretches voluptuously. The aristocracy gathers in the plush restaurants for two-hour repasts. Tourists jostle on the narrow streets beneath the balconies of iron filigree. In a crowded, smoky club maracas seethe a snaky whisper, and a girl with long, silken black hair and purple-shadowed eyes stands in a dark doorway like a carnivorous flower waiting for prey.

The apartment was still unlocked. I didn't like that. I turned the lights on, and I liked the emptiness even less.

I decided to go downstairs to see if I could get a lead on the direction she'd taken.

Just as I opened the door, a peeled-egg head showed in the stairwell, a bulbous moon catching the feeble hallway light.

He came up with slow, deliberate movements. He was a big guy with a fleshy, quietly humorous face. His name was Steve Ivey. He was a lieutenant of detectives. He was far from being a flashy man. Maybe he wasn't even brilliant. But he was a good cop, determined, with an integrity that was bone deep.

He saw me standing in the doorway, paused, and came forward slowly.

"Hello, Ed."

I returned the greeting.

"Going out?" he asked.

"Just coming in. How goes it?"

"Hot," he said.

"You didn't come here to discuss the weather."

"I'm looking for somebody. A little doll named Tina La Flor. You know her."

"Sure."

"She came out of this building a couple hours ago."

"What makes you think that?" I fished with a bland face. His was just as bland.

"Well, we put out a call on her. The beat cop over here remembers he saw her a couple hours ago. Coming out of the building. Can't help but spot and remember a little doll like that."

"I guess not. But why me? There are a lot of people in the building. She might have been visiting any of them."

Ivey made a pad of his handkerchief and wiped his bald dome. "That's true. But I got a hunch she came here because she needed help. Private-cop help. And there's only one private cop in the building."

"She isn't here now," I said. "You want to come in and look around?"

"Where is she?"

"I don't know."

"What did she tell you two hours ago?"

"She didn't tell me anything, Steve. I wasn't here." It was clear that Ivey didn't, as yet, know Tina had come to the apartment last night. His only connection of her to me was her departure for dinner. I didn't see any sense in tying knots until I found out which way the rope was dangling.

"Mind telling me where you were?"

"Yes, I do mind," I said. "I didn't see Tina La Flor this afternoon, and that's the truth."

Ivey placidly lighted a cigar. "You're up to something, Rivers. When you get that dumb-ape look, it means you've turned on that computer under your skull. What's with Tina La Flor?"

"I've told you. . . ."

"How'd you get those marks on your cheek?"

"I had to go downtown last night and check a shorted burglar alarm. When I got back, a mugger jumped me."

"You didn't report it."

"He didn't get anything. I chased him."

"You should have reported him."

"I didn't get a look at him. It was too dark."

"Okay," Ivey shrugged, "if that's the way you citizens want it. If Tina La Flor shows up, will you let me know?"

"Maybe. Why would she come here?"

"Probably to retain you. Over in her neighborhood a little while ago some kids at after-dinner play noticed an open window in Tina La Flor's cottage. You know how kids are. The place was dark, and they decided to sneak in and have a look at all that miniature furniture they'd heard their parents talk about.

"But the cottage wasn't empty, Ed. A big guy, all bloody, was lying in the living room. One of the kids, a little girl, she got hysterical just from the sight of it and the family doctor had to put her under sedation."

Grisly sweat crawled down my chest. "Somebody beat the guy up?"

"Somebody killed the guy," Ivey said. "He'd taken a beating. The blow that seems to have finished him came from a blackjack we found near the body."

The butterflies in my belly turned to writhing snakes. "Know who he is?"

"Fellow named Bucks Jordan," Ivey said. "A quick routine on him turned up a record. Vicious, dirty, petty stuff. Beating up a woman, attempted extortion. He worked a carny for awhile—along with Tina Fa Flor."

"Coincidence," I said. "You can connect two thirds of the ex-carny people in this town through past show employment."

"Wasn't coincidence that he was found in her cottage," Ivey said doggedly.

"But you can't think that a little dame like her could slug a . . ."

"I'm thinking she could hire it done," Ivey said, "whatever the reasons. And when it was done too thoroughly and she saw she had a fresh corpse on her hands, I'm thinking she'd figure she needed some help and needed it desperately."

"Which brings you to me." I wondered if my lips looked as stiff as they felt.

"Which brought *her* to you," Ivey corrected. "Now you know. You'll contact me if she shows up?"

"I'll keep in touch," I said.

I stood in the hallway until Ivey disappeared in the stairwell. Then I went in the apartment, closed the door, and fell back against it.

Someone had entered the cottage, found Bucks' own blackjack, and used it for a final blow.

That's the way it had to be. I knew he'd been alive when I left.

And yet—the question seeped smotheringly through my mind.

No, I told myself, I didn't kill him. He was alive.

Then who knew he was there? Who killed him?

I went to the kitchenette and broke out a beer. It tasted like ipecac.

One part of me raged to another part: Damn it, I *know* I didn't kill Bucks Jordan.

And the other part whispered back: Even if you didn't try and tell it to Ivey.

The phone screamed.

I went in the bed-sittingroom and picked the phone up.

"Ed?"

"Tina—where the devil are you?"

"Why'd you do it, Ed?"

"You think that I . . ."

"I heard, just now, on a newscast . . . Ed, I didn't want you to get him off my neck with such permanence. But don't worry," she sobbed. "I won't say a thing, even if they catch me."

"Tina . . ."

"I won't let you down, Ed."

"Tina!"

She hung up.

Chapter Five

What's more, she disappeared.

Operating on about four hours sleep, I used up most of the next day without getting a lead on Tina. I found out several facts that did seem to back up her story. She did have a new agent, a New Yorker who'd caught her act while vacationing in Florida. A long distance call to him confirmed that he had hopes of selling Tina in the big time.

The day turned up a few personal details relating to Tina.

Her parents had abandoned her when, as a kid, it appeared certain she had stopped growing and was destined to be a freak.

In any slum, there are children of questionable parentage. The slum area of Ybor City was no exception. The homeless kid had attached herself to a couple named Cardezas. Without officially adopting her, Mr. and Mrs. Cardezas shared their bean pot and sausage roll with Tina.

In later years, the Cardezas had four children of their own who attached no particular importance to Tina's size because she'd always been that way to them.

In late afternoon, I drove out to the Cardezas house.

It was a cramped, unpainted structure with a drooping front porch. On a street of such houses, a street swarming with noisy kids, the house was faintly lopsided on its cement block pillars, as if a long-ago hurricane had nudged it hard.

My new car drew looks from laboring men with empty lunch pails. No husband would return to the Cardezas house. An animal handler, he'd been killed two years ago while trying to handle his charges during a circus fire.

I crossed the hard-packed yard and knocked on the flimsy door. When opened, the door framed a big, warm, bosomy woman of middle age. Her thick hair was in jet coils, stranded with silver, about her head. Her face was full and fleshy and smiling. I suspected that the smile was a natural expression. It gave a glow to the big, open face, which was dusted with misty perspiration, and extended to the large, liquid eyes of striking black.

She was dressed in simple cotton and held half a dozen dinner plates in the crook of her arm.

"Mrs. Cardezas?"

"Yes?"

"My name is Ed Rivers."

"Oh, I know of you. Please come in."

I glanced at the dinner plates. She laughed. "Oh, that can wait. Or perhaps you'd eat with us?"

In the house behind her, a young voice said, "Bang, bang, you're dead, Miguel!" And another screeched, "No, I'm not, you missed!" And the first yelled, "Mama, make Miguel play right!"

Mrs. Cardezas called over her shoulder, "Miguel, you must die when properly shot. Now some manners out of you! We have company."

She stepped aside for me to enter. "Poor Miguel," she clucked. "Always he is the one to get shot."

I stepped into a living room that was barren, but clean. On a table against the far wall rested a large Bible. Over the table hung a crucifix.

"Are you looking for Tina, Mr. Rivers?" Mrs. Cardezas asked as she sat on the edge of a wicker chair and rested the plates on her knees.

"Yes. How did you know?"

"I only suspected. She said she was going to you for advice —about that one. That Bucks Jordan."

"You know that Jordan is dead?"

"Oh, yes. I heard." She nodded toward the dilapidated television set in the corner. As if that were a signal, an olive-skinned, black-haired girl of seven or eight skipped into the room. With a curtsey of apology she crossed in front of me and turned the set on.

"*Muchacha,*" Mrs. Cardezas said quietly, "we have a guest."

"But I'm hungry, mama, and . . ."

"The television will not feed you."

"But, mama . . ."

"And neither will your rudeness hurry your dinner. To the kitchen with you!"

"Yes, mama."

Mrs. Cardezas returned her attention to me. "I heard that he was found in her cottage," she said, a sudden heaviness in her voice. "Poor Tina. Always the life so hard. And with the big heart. The little income from my husband's death— it is not enough. Tina provides us the rest. Did you know?"

"No, I didn't."

"I must stay home with the children," she said. "This is only right for the children. Children should not be abandoned even while a mother works. Tina would take us from here, but I refuse. I accept what I must. That is all. We have a good home, good food, good love. Tina is . . . Oh, you must help Tina, Mr. Rivers!"

"I want to, but I've got to find her first. Can you tell me where she is?"

"Ah, if I only could. . . . That one. Jordan. You must find his enemy, Mr. Rivers. We will find a way of paying."

"When did you last see Tina?"

"Two days ago. She was upset, talking of going to you."

"And Jordan? What did she say about him?"

"A very bad man."

"Only that?"

"What more to say for him?" she shrugged.

"Nothing about his connections? What he was doing?"

"He worked on the boat."

"The *Sprite?*"

"*Si.* Yes, that is it. The girl there, she chased Bucks. Would that she had caught him!"

"Is her name D. D.?"

"I do not know, Mr. Rivers. Tina said she was the daughter of the owner."

She followed me to the door, repeating her invitation to dinner.

The aroma of her cooking was a spicy temptation. "Thanks," I said, "but I'll grab a sandwich. I'm going to be busy."

She laid her hand over mine. "I'm glad Tina has such a friend as you, Mr. Rivers. I feel better now."

I wasn't too sure of the friendship bit, not until I learned what omissions, if any, Tina had made when she suckered me into a job that resulted in a corpse. I hoped Tina was as clean as Mrs. Cardezas thought.

I nodded and let it go at that. There was no point in telling her that I was working primarily for myself, or that no other client's interests had ever been so close to my heart, Tina not excepted.

The sun was scalding the Gulf and bleeding all over the western horizon when I got to the bait camp.

The leathery, sinewy young proprietor padded the length of the plank pier, preceding me. He slipped the line on a flat-bottom.

"Is Miss Lessard out there?" I asked, motioning with my head toward the *Sprite.*

"Could be," he said. He kept the line taut as I stepped into the boat. When I picked up the oars, he pitched the line into the hull.

I pointed at the skiff bobbing a couple slips away. Weathered letters spelled *Sprite* on the small boat. "She didn't come ashore in one of the schooner's small boats?"

"Look, mister," he said, scratching his naked, bony chest, "I don't keep track of their comings and goings." He spat over the edge of the pier, wiped his hands on the seat of his jeans. "Snug her up when you come in. I'll prob'ly be over to the house."

In my control, the flat-bottom was a cantankerous jackass with a perverted sense of humor. She balked and rolled as I wrestled her out to the *Sprite*.

I let the sloppy job of rowing give me the angle I wanted, a stern view of the schooner. The lettering was faded, the lighting none too good.

I made out the registry. The *Sprite's* home port was below the equator, in Peru.

I splashed the flat-bottom to the starboard hull, grabbed the ladder, snubbed the line, and climbed aboard. A radio was softly emitting dance music from the cabin.

I called out, "Hello, the *Sprite*."

A girl came out of the cabin. The deepening, hot twilight sizzled with shock. I thought she was wearing only her birthday suit. Then I saw that the color of her playsuit did it, a deep tan like her skin.

She was tall, supple and sinewy, but she didn't have a pared-down look. The flare, swell, rise and fall of the curves of her body added up to an impression of sinuousness that was almost illegal. She had ash blonde hair, short cut, tousled about her small face.

She studied me gravely, not saying anything.

"May I come aboard?" I asked.

She giggled without losing her mock gravity. "Aren't you already?"

"I like to have permission," I said. "Is Mr. Lessard here?"

"Nope."

"Are you D. D.?"

"For sure now." Her voice suggested birth and childhood in southeastern United States, not Peru. She started forward, stubbed the toe of her guaraches, grabbed the rail. She stood holding the support with both hands and giggled again.

"I'm afraid you'll have to help me," she said. "It's a damn stormy sea."

She smiled as I neared her. She had a broad mouth, very red lips, nice teeth. Her forehead crinkled as she worked at getting her green eyes in focus.

"Where have we met?" she asked.

"We haven't."

The fumes of hard liquor made a heavy incense about her. "You a seaman?"

"No."

"You look like one. Like a big, ugly Spick or Portugee first mate on a rusty tub out of Dakar or some place. You sure we haven't met?"

"Certain, I'm sorry to say."

Her eyes crossed a little. "We can remedy that, can't we? I'm Miss Delphelia Dorchester Lessard—ain't it hell? Better known as D. D. Lately of Virginia, suh, Bora Bora, Capetown, Peru and a backwater town or two. Who might you be?"

Her brows quirked as she got the images of me unfuzzed and melted together.

"The name is Rivers," I said. "Ed to my friends."

She straightened, took aim with her green eyes, and headed for the foredeck without assistance. She made it to a chair, dropped into it, and gasped. "There! But now I'm away from the cabin and drinking liquor. Will you be a pal and fetch me a drink if I need one?"

"Sure."

"Then you're Ed to me. Golden friend. Good old Ed. You married, Ed?"

"No."

"Me neither. It stinks."

"Sometimes maybe."

"All the time, old friend. There's always a kid or two. They got no choice. Any dirty crud can be a father, and the kid's got no say-so. Let's pass a law, Ed."

"Okay. What kind?"

"Giving kids the choice of cruds for a father. Or maybe you don't agree?"

"Why not?"

"You're working for Alex, aren't you? Isn't that why you came here?"

"Honey, you can feel as you like about your old man."

"Thanks, pal. What's your official capacity in our little party?"

I hesitated. "Your father wanted Bucks Jordan located."

"I'll say!" She gave me a goofy grin that managed to be cute. "The local talent looks capable. You capable, Ed?"

"I try to be."

"Where is Bucks?"

I searched her face. She had trouble keeping me in focus. She seemed to be one of those with a cell, deep in the gray matter, that continues to function even when alcohol has turned the rest of the anatomy to rubber.

I decided she hadn't heard. She would have remembered, drunk as she was.

"In the morgue," I said.

Chapter Six

She sat thinking about it for so long that I began to wonder if she'd heard me.

Then she said in a sobered tone, "You're not working for Alex at all. You're a cop, aren't you?"

"I give you my word, sweetheart. . . ."

"I don't think I'd better talk to you any more until Alex gets back."

Her mind was made up. That small, cute chin had a stubborn tilt.

"All right," I said. "I'll level with you. I was, in a way, working for your father. I was trying to locate Bucks and came out here to inquire around. Mr. Lessard asked me to let him know if I found Bucks."

"So you found him."

"No. Somebody else found him in the way that you mean."

"Then why trouble yourself further?"

"I'm a private detective. I have my reasons."

"I'll bet you have." I saw anxiety growing in her eyes. She stood up with much difficulty. "Go away," she said, "you got no business here."

"You don't seem very put out by Bucks' death."

"Why should I? He was another crud."

"You didn't seem to feel that way about him."

She stood swaying, holding the back of the deck chair with one hand. "Now who in hell could have told you that? A Tampa female he was trying to make jealous?"

"Was there room for jealousy?"

39

"Oh, cripes, he thought every woman was gone on him. I annoyed him a little because I was bored."

"The Tampa police might like to hear about it."

"You're not scaring me any, old pal Ed."

"That sounds like a denial."

She moved away from the chair. Her mind mustered dignity, but her legs refused to go along. She tipped toward the rail.

When I sprang and caught her, she screamed softly. The sensuous contours of her lithe body writhed around. Her nails flashed across my cheek.

She wheeled away dizzily, came in contact with the rail, and pinwheeled over the side.

I rushed to the rail and looked at the darkening water. The last drops of the shower caused by her fall rasped back to the surface.

As the water stilled, I saw the shadow of her under the surface. She was rising slowly, limply.

I plunged in feet first, grabbed her around the waist when the water quit roaring over me. Threshing, I somehow got us both to the surface. Gagging on sea water, blowing it out of my nose, I used a combination of dog-paddle and dirty wrestling tactics against the water.

I made it the few feet to the ladder, grabbed and held on. The dead weight of her draped across my forearm tried to pull us back. As soon as I got breath, I decided she was lighter in the water.

I ducked under, shoved her across my shoulder, and pulled again at the ladder. The rope stretched with a small sound like clean, thoroughly rinsed hair.

I hoisted her on deck, stretched her out face down. She didn't need artificial respiration. Already she was groaning sickly.

She turned over slowly and looked up at me. Droplets of water were on her face, her lashes. With the playsuit plastered to her, it was hard to keep my mind on business.

I kneeled beside her and picked her up. She lay against me in limp exhaustion, arms and legs dangling. The liquor and shock of the water had sapped her. With the dew of the warm, salty bay on her face, she looked vulnerable and incredibly tired.

I moved aft, stooped, and carried her down the hatchway. There was a lounge of sorts, a small galley, and beyond that a companionway. The first door I tried was locked. The second opened as my fingers, extended from under her, turned the knob.

I pushed the door with my foot. The cabin was small, with a bunk down one side, a built-in sort of combination dressing table and storage compartment down the other. The single porthole stood open. An exhaust fan was humming softly somewhere in the boat, bringing a continuous wash of air from outside.

I placed D. D. on the bunk and stepped back to get my breath. A glanced showed me that the cabin was like the rest of the schooner, worn from hard usage and lacking in the finer points of meticulous care, but sound and serviceable.

"Thanks," she said, very quietly.

"What did you expect me to do? Where are some towels?"

"There. That top drawer."

I got out a towel, pitched it to her, and helped myself to a second.

She acted as if she wanted to sit up, but she was too weak.

"Maybe you need a doctor," I suggested.

"Nope. Another drink will get the old corpuscles in motion."

"Don't you think . . ."

"Uh-uh, Ed. No lectures. You just saved my life. Want to kill me by refusing me a drink?"

"I'll go topside and dry out," I said. "Give you a chance to change. You can get your own drink."

"Mean old bear, aren't you?" She was able to giggle again.

I went on deck, took off my shirt, and wrung it out. I

pressed my wallet between folds of the towel. The rest of my clothes would have to dry where they were. I used the towel to dry my face, arms, back, and chest, and then I put the shirt on again.

I heard the scuff of her footsteps. I turned and saw her coming forward. She'd put on a light blouse and skirt: In the early darkness she looked wan, pale, the ash blonde hair still limp about her face.

I looked at the drink in her hand. "Trying to fall down dead in that stuff?"

"Would it matter to you?"

"For some strange reason, yes. You remind me of somebody. Some quality the two of you have in common. Her name is Tina."

"Is she beautiful?" D. D. asked.

"Very much. She's a show girl—all three feet of her."

I caught the change in her face. She turned and moved toward a deck chair. I took her arm and put enough pressure on to force her to face me.

"Where is she, D. D.?"

"I don't know what you're talking about."

"You were jarred when I mentioned her."

She laughed. It sounded weak and forced. "No—I was thinking of a kid three feet tall being a show girl."

"She's a midget."

"Oh?"

"Knew Bucks Jordan," I said.

She yielded beyond the pressure of my hand, her body sliding toward me. The touch of her length against mine was firm but pliant. There was an aura about her like the warm damp of the tropical water whispering against the hull of the *Sprite*.

"If you're trying to parboil me," I said, "you're making a fine start."

"Good," she murmured. Her arms slid around my neck.

Tampa, cops and a possible murder rap faded to the dark

side of the moon. The green eyes were half closed, the lips parted. My breathing clogged up.

Then I reached and took her wrists in my hands and broke her grip.

"Only I keep thinking about Bucks," I said, "and the fact that he came to this boat, then deserted it, then ended up dead."

D. D. showed no embarrassment in being rebuffed, no anger, no scorn. She looked at me a moment. Then she pulled herself away, walked to the deck chair, and sat down. She still had the remains of the drink in her hand. She studied it briefly before she killed it.

The raw liquor brought a small cough from her. "You know something," she said in a liquor-strangled tone, "you're old-fashioned, that's what. Furthermore, you're a damn fool. On top of that, I don't like your insinuations. My father and I are not murderers. We're . . . I guess you could call us vagabonds. We wander as we damn please. Maybe the Shangri-la we're looking for isn't on the face of this earth. But that's our own business, isn't it?"

She looked at me over the empty glass. "We came here as tourists, pure and simple. Bucks worked for us briefly. Then he quit. We haven't seen him since."

"All pure and simple," I said.

"That's right—and you can get the hell off this boat, Ed, or should I say Mr. Rivers?"

"Maybe I'll stick around and talk to your father."

"Alex will tell you the same thing I have."

"I don't doubt that, D. D. But I'd like to hear it from him. There might be a minor variation or two."

"Not tonight," she said. "Over the side with you, or I'll radio the authorities."

She set the glass beside the chair. She stood up. Maybe it was the liquor, or she was dredging deep into her reserves. The weakness in her was gone now.

I went over the side and got in the flat-bottom. As I cast off, I looked up at her. She'd followed me to the rail.

"Ed. . . ."

I sat holding the oars while the skiff drifted a few feet.

"Ed, thanks anyhow for fishing me out of the drink."

"Any time," I said.

As I rowed in, I reflected on the fact that she could have phrased it differently, taken a completely opposite mental attitude and point of view. After all, if I hadn't gone out to the *Sprite*, she never would have fallen overboard and endangered her life in the first place.

I docked the flat-bottom, walked down the rickety wooden pier, and spotted a light under the pines thirty yards or so away.

The light came from a weathered, frame cottage that was mostly screened-in porch. At a table on the porch the bait camp operator was wolfing fish and hush-puppies, washing the grub down with coffee from a thick mug. He was still clothed only in jeans and sneakers. I wondered if he'd ever had a shirt on.

Swarms of mosquitoes welting my hands and face, I knocked on the screen door. The proprietor belched comfortably, got to his feet, and picked up a newspaper from a pile of magazines on an old rattan chair.

He cracked the door, reached out with the newspaper, and scared the mosquitoes off. Then he told me to come in.

He took in my rumpled condition. "You lost my boat?"

"No, it's snugged in the slip."

"That's good." He returned to the table and resumed eating, having a wonderful time with handfuls of greasy mullet.

He stopped eating when I moved to the table and shoved my identification under his nose. "Ed Rivers, the private cop. I've heard of you. Regular Tampa landmark, ain't you. Only I told you the first time you was here, I don't know nothing about the *Sprite* or the people on her. The water's for free. She can anchor where she likes."

"You're not at all curious."

"Nope. Don't pay."

"The *Sprite* came from Peru."

"Did she?"

"Not by herself," I said.

"Don't seem likely, does it?"

"There had to be a crew. Must be a deckhand or two kicking around someplace."

He continued eating, digging chunks of white flesh of mullet with his fingers and shoving them into the fish oil smear of his mouth. "I figure they're Americans on the boat, or foreign folks with the right papers. Ain't heard of no law getting broke. Don't believe in poking my nose, neither."

I creased a twenty dollar bill and laid it beside his plate. A brown lump of hush-puppy stopped halfway to his mouth.

"Two fellows," he said. "They were on the *Sprite* when she dropped anchor."

"Do you know their names?"

"Heard them talking. Kincaid and Smith."

"Where are they now?"

"Don't know." He slid the twenty off the table. "They came ashore the day after she anchored. Way they acted, I figured they'd been in ship's quarters long enough. Wanted pavement under their feet and bright lights around them."

"When was that?"

"Couple weeks ago. Maybe longer. I think it was on a Thursday. You know how it is. Same hot sun, same sky day after day. Time don't mean much."

"Have they been back?"

He nodded. "Now and then."

"Like on a schedule?"

"How would I know?"

"What do they look like?"

"I dunno. Just a couple guys." He thought for a moment. "Dressed okay, talked polite. But tough. Not in the mouth or walk where it don't count. Tough."

"You know the Scanlons?"

"I've seen them." He pinched up the last flecks of mullet. "They go out to the *Sprite* regular."

"They didn't come in on her?"

"Nope. Showed up the day she got in, though."

"Sounds like," I said, "they came from some place else, arriving here specifically to meet the *Sprite*."

He grunted. He'd had his quota of talking for a week.

Chapter Seven

Maria Scanlon was waiting beside my car, a dumpy, drab figure in the early evening.

"I recognized your car, Mr. Rivers," she explained with a motion of her hand. "I wanted to see you. I've been trying to call your office."

"What's on your mind?"

"Why . . . Bucks Jordan—and you." Her sturdiness of stance misfired. She looked lonely. On her face was an unhealthy eagerness.

"I wanted to give you a chance to explain," she said. She licked her lips. Her eyes glinted with a sensual willingness to partake of the troubles of a world gone wrong.

"Lady, I don't follow you."

"Don't be afraid," she coaxed.

"But there's no explanation to make."

She laid her hand on my arm. "You can trust me. You were looking for Bucks. A little later I heard on the newscasts that he was dead, beaten to death." She leaned toward me and I automatically leaned back. "Were you forced to fight for your life?"

"The last time I saw you, Mrs. Scanlon, you were defending Bucks."

"Alex was being unjust to him. But Bucks is dead now."

"Beyond help."

"Yes. He doesn't have to be vicious any longer." She let her hand slide down my arm and fall at her side. "Once he had the innocence of a child, like the rest of us. As you yourself had. Life has put some rough edges on you. . . . Oh,

47

they're very visible to me. But it isn't too late. If you were defending yourself. . . ."

"Do you know why I wanted to see Bucks?"

"I suspect the reason," she said. "He must have had something you wanted." Unconsciously, her gaze flicked toward the dark hulk of the *Sprite* riding silently in the bay.

"You know what he took off the schooner?" I asked.

"I'm not aware. . . ."

"Kincaid and Smith were after the same thing. Two of them looking for Bucks, weren't they?"

"Kincaid and Smith . . . You know them?"

"Come on," I said coldly. "Bucks made the heist and the panthers were set loose. Where are they now?"

"I think you're confused."

"Then you better clear me on a point or two," I said.

She wheeled and started away. I grabbed her arm harder than I intended and jerked her toward me. She grimaced and half-kneeled in sudden pain. "I understand," she said softly. "It's the mode of action that's been instilled in you."

"Get off the pink cloud, Maria, and start talking."

"You're wrong," she said. "You're acting very wrongly."

"Kincaid and Smith," I said.

"I wanted to help you, to understand. But I can't reach you, can I?"

"Yes, and you're tiring me."

"I won't hold this against you," she said. She remained in that bent-over position, accepting the pressure on her arm, absorbing pain. Her face twisted up to me. Her eyes held a peculiar light of joy, as if in this moment she found a sense of sacrifice and satisfaction. Her passive resistance had the quality of a cloying, enveloping fog, which cannot be driven back by throwing your fists into it.

I shoved her away. "For your information, I didn't kill Bucks. So don't waste your sympathy on me."

"Pity is never wasted, Mr. Rivers." She turned quickly and walked away.

I hesitated; then I went around to the driver's side of the car.

As I opened the door, I heard footsteps approaching. A man said, "Hey, you."

I turned. He was a tall, rangy, rawboned man of about thirty. He had a lazy, lean face and jet-black hair that gleamed in the half light.

He took a final hard pull on his cigarette, dropped it, and ground it in the sand.

"Your name Rivers?" He had a deep-South accent.

"That's right."

"I thought I saw my wife over here."

"Mrs. Scanlon? You did."

He slipped his fingers under his belt and stood with his arms crooked. I've seen southern farmers and hillbillies in the identical position. His eyes were a lazy mask.

"I'm Jack Scanlon," he said.

"Pleased to know you."

"Yeah," he said flatly. "What was she talking about?"

"Bucks Jordan."

"Yeah," he laughed. "Her latest missionary project."

"Late is the word."

"That's right, isn't it? She's always got one. Once she dressed a tramp up and took him to the Court of The Two Sisters for dinner. But she's a good kid in spite of it."

He looked in the direction she had taken. "Only don't take anything she says serious."

"Thanks, I won't."

"You're the fellow looking for Bucks, weren't you?"

"That's right."

"Only somebody beat you to him."

"It looks like it."

"So now what are you looking for?"

I looked at him. He looked at me. We measured each other. He found amusement from some source and expressed it in a laugh. "Whatever it is, you won't find it here."

"I've got plenty of time," I said.

"Well, now, a man never knows for sure about those things."

He gave me a mock salute as a good-by gesture and moved away without apparent hurry.

I heard the echo of footsteps on the wooden pier, then the dip of oars as a small boat went sliding out to the *Sprite*.

The schooner, I decided, wasn't as sound as I'd thought at first. There were worms in the woodwork. I had a hunch they'd be quiescent for a short spell, waiting and watching, forming a decision. Then the worms would show some fangs.

My discomfort right then wasn't due wholly to the starchy stiffness of my salty, dried clothes. I yearned for some bosom buddies named Lieutenant Steve Ivey and the Tampa police department.

The people of the *Sprite* had easy, simple explanations. The schooner was here legally, no real oddity in these waters. There was no law against the Scanlons coming to town to meet their friends, the Lessards. Bucks Jordan's contact with the *Sprite* had been brief. He'd worked a little and quit, right in keeping with his known character.

Even with anxiety adding wishfulness to my thinking, I had to admit that Ivey would find nothing in these people to offset the fact that I'd been the last to see Bucks alive, after clobbering him.

It was just me and the worms. And I was tired and hungry and needed a beer.

In fresh clothes, I ate sandwiches and sipped the beer while I talked on the phone in my apartment with Sergeant Gonzales at headquarters.

We jawed the usual hellos and how-goes-it, and then I said, "I got an out-of-town client who wants some information on a man who just turned up here. Can help?"

"Can, Ed. What's his name?"

"Scanlon. Jack Scanlon."

"I'll call you back."

"Fine. By the way, you turn up Tina La Flor yet?"

"Still looking. It's as bad as if she'd growed up, all of a sudden, and we didn't recognize her no more."

My face moistened. "How about the Bucks Jordan thing?"

"What's your interest, Ed?"

"Well, the kid—Tina—she's a friend of mine. Steve was around here looking for her. I'm naturally curious."

"It's all in the newspapers."

"Dead end?"

"So far."

"I'll stick to the phone for the Scanlon thing," I said.

Gonzales called back a few minutes later. "We got nothing on a Jack Scanlon, Ed."

I thanked him, sat staring at the phone. People usually say more than they know they're saying—if you keep your ears open for details.

After a minute, it began to come through in the case of Jack Scanlon. He'd mentioned the Court of the Two Sisters, a restaurant in New Orleans.

I picked up the phone. I caught Nationwide's New Orleans agent at home and told him what I wanted.

In an hour, he had it. Jack Scanlon was all over the New Orleans police blotter. Trigger man. Strong-arm boy. Hoodlum deluxe.

"He's been in and out of trouble since he was fourteen," my New Orleans sidekick told me. "You name it, he's been suspected of it. At one time or another he has been, and I quote: Collector for a loan shark. Enforcer for a protection racket. Personal bodyguard for a crooked gambler.

" 'Maturing, he worked his way up. Suspected of syndicate connections. Drifted to Central America. Deported from one of our Latin neighbors after an abortive revolt. He was lucky to escape a firing squad.

" 'Not long after he first appeared in New Orleans he was picked up on suspicion of murder. Released for lack of evidence.' "

"Nice guy," I said.

"And slippery, my beer-chugging pal. Scanlon has a long record of arrests, some time in jail, but only one conviction on a felony. Several years ago he beat up an old lady, nearly killing her, after she squawked about the loan shark's interest rates. This was in Illinois. A shyster got him off with the minimum.

"The department psychologist here classes him as a constitutional psychopathic inferior—which means that he knows right from wrong but doesn't give a damn. Good or evil evoke none of the usual reactions in him, although he can differentiate the two. He'd as soon kill you as look at you."

"Keep cheering me up," I said bleakly.

"Nearly a year ago, he married a drab named Maria Blake, an oddball who used to hang around the bistros in the Quarter, where she must have met him.

"The headquarters boys here in New Orleans say that it was a real surprise. She was a frump in the sex department, but that wasn't the point. The fact that he married was the point in itself. Scanlon, like a lot of his breed, seemed to have a real aversion to women. He was never in their company. Mostly, they felt something in his presence that caused them to shy away from him. It was almost as if he had a horror of the female anatomy.

"She comes from an excellent old family. They'd shunted her from one private school to another summer camp all her life. She was the awkward, graceless ball of fat who never fitted. I'd guess she despised them, and the feeling was mutual. They disowned her promptly after she married Scanlon and she moved into a rat-hole with him living like a real bum."

"When did they leave New Orleans?"

"No one here is sure. Recently, it just dawned on some of the boys here that they hadn't seen Scanlon around for a while. What's up over there, Ed?"

"I'll let you know," I said, "when I find out."

After I hung up, I stood at the window, mulling over everything I'd learned so far. I thought of Scanlon's experience in Central America, and of Lessard's registry of a boat in Peru. The two had met here, where Ybor City provided a nerve end to Latin America.

I locked the apartment and went down to the narrow, sweltering street. A man came from the direction of the all-night market down on the corner, a bag of groceries in his arm.

I headed for the alley to go around and get my car. The man with the groceries smiled and nodded. He was about fifty, big and powerful, dressed neatly in an inexpensive tropical suit.

He shifted to block my way, showed me the heavy revolver in his free hand, nestled close to the groceries. I saw that the gun was silenced.

I stood on sharp tacks for a second. He had a big, broad, pleasantly dumb face, brush-cut, iron-gray hair. He looked like a hearty fellow all washed up after a day working in the oil fields or driving a bulldozer. He had made a calm, matter-of-fact decision. I saw it in his slate-gray eyes. The decision involved the gun.

"What do you want?" I said, watching for a flicker of uncertainty in the decision.

"You."

"Which are you?" I stalled.

"Which?"

"Kincaid or Smith?"

He didn't change expression. "Smith. You want to die this close to the gutter?"

"No," I said, "not tonight."

Chapter Eight

Smith revealed his experience in such activities in the way he herded me in the alley. He stayed about three paces behind me. It gave him time and space to use the gun, even if I'd been the fastest fool on earth.

I heard the groceries slide down his body, thunk on the crushed shell paving of the alley.

"Keep moving," he said.

As I passed down the scabby brick profile of the building, there was a change in the sound of the footsteps behind me. I glanced over my shoulder. I guessed it was Kincaid who'd slithered out of the shadows to join Smith.

"Stop," Smith said. "Right there."

I stopped, in the exposed, most open part of the alley where it widened at the car shed.

Kincaid circled cautiously, coming in behind me. He was as tall as Smith, not as heavy. He moved lithely, a man of perfect reflexes and coordination. The after-glow in the alley from the street didn't give me much of a look at his face. I got an impression of hard bone and sharp angles, with the eyes set under a high forehead.

"Put your hands on your head, Rivers," Smith said.

I caressed my thinning crown.

Behind me, Kincaid's hands started at my ankles. He passed up my wallet. Reaching in my side pocket, he appropriated my keys. Then he lifted the .38 from under my lightweight jacket.

The sheath of my knife was a comforting touch between my shoulder blades.

"I've been wanting to meet you," I said.

"We've shared the desire," Kincaid said behind me. He had a low, crisp voice. Each word was well enunciated. I wondered if he'd ever conned his way into reasonably cultured circles. "Our inquiries regarding you, Rivers, have been thorough, if discreet. For one thing," he laughed softly, "we heard a rumor about a knife, a flat piece of steel honed to razor sharpness."

His hand jerked the collar of my jacket. My shoulders reacted, snapping the collar tight on his fingers. My right hand dropped from the crown of my head, clamped on his wrist. At the same time, the rest of my body was in motion. I collapsed against Kincaid as the gun in Smith's hand coughed. The lighting was bad, and he was afraid of hitting his partner. The slug whined off the brick wall behind us.

With Kincaid off balance, I used my legs like steel springs. He gasped as the top of my head slammed up against his chin.

I spun Kincaid as Smith sprang to one side to get in another shot. Without breaking motion, I pile-drivered the reeling Kincaid at Smith. The three of us collided. Kincaid went to his knees. Tripping over him, I grabbed for Smith's gun. Smith was tearing himself free of the melee, trying to keep his footing.

Smith's backward moving bulk and my grip on his wrist threw my weight against Kincaid. He went prone, threshing and grabbing at me. Kicking at Kincaid, I kept the direction of motion constant against Smith.

Smith tripped, tottered backwards. His face was a slick, white smear in the night. His gun wrist was slippery as he threw his bulk behind the effort to bring the gun to bear.

Sprawling toward Smith, I tried to get a steady footing. His free hand was a fist, slugging at my face. I turtled my head between my shoulders. His knuckles cracked on my forehead. The alley tilted for a second.

I butted Smith in the belly. I sensed his heels catching in

the loose shell paving. He clubbed at me with his fists as we reeled on insecure footing. The blows struck my shoulders and back. I stayed with him like a babe clinging to its mother.

Then Kincaid's weight hit me from behind. The three of us went down in a tangle of stabbing arms and legs. I heard the breath grunt out of Smith. His grip on the gun weakened.

Kincaid grabbed my hair and tried to jerk me loose from Smith. I took the eye-watering punishment, my knee in Smith's groin. A sharp hiss of pain came from him.

I was gambling on them being unwilling to risk an un-silenced shot in the alley. I was right about that. I almost had the silenced gun ripped from Smith's fingers, the authority to command.

Then Kincaid collected his senses, cooled his head. He ceased his ineffectual attack on my back. I felt his weight leave me. My skull split open. He'd taken aim and done a perfect place kick.

The night was an empty sinkhole, draining my strength. I felt Smith writhing from under me, but there wasn't a thing I could do about it.

The two of them stood over me a few moments, getting their wind back, the toe of Kincaid's shoe touching me now and then in grim speculation.

"Well," Kincaid said, pulling breath into his lungs, "we heard he was a tough old grizzly."

"Yeah," Smith said in a thick voice.

"The way you're supposed to be tough," Kincaid said.

"I didn't expect . . ."

"I know," Kincaid said, "but he saw it as his last chance, and what did he have to lose?"

"I'll fix him for it," Smith said. "I'll fix him good. I'll make him wish he'd never got greedy with Bucks Jordan."

"You'll do what I tell you to do," Kincaid said. "And next time you shoot off a gun with me that close around, I'm going to make you eat it."

"Now, Kincaid, you know I . . ."

"I know you get rattled. You should have kept your head, slugged him with the gun. It would have spared us much."

Dimly, I heard the slapping of his hands as Kincaid brushed himself off. "I should charge you for this suit."

"We'll get plenty of suits when we finish dredging Rivers," Smith said.

"Ha, ha," Kincaid said sarcastically.

"I thought it was pretty good," Smith's tone echoed rebuff.

"At least we've got him now," Kincaid said. "And I'll be sore in every muscle and joint for a week because of it. Put him in the car and let's get out of here before some wandering joker puts an end to our run of luck."

Weak as a half-drowned dog, I lay and took it as Smith put his knee in the small of my back and jerked my hands behind me.

"Lend me your necktie, Kincaid."

He used the tie to lash my hands. Then he, slid his own soiled handkerchief to make a gag. With the dirty linen tearing my jaws, I really began to hate Smith.

He grunted as he clutched my shoulders and dragged me toward my own car. He stuffed me in the back seat, got under the wheel, and Kincaid slid in beside him.

Every movement of the car jolted through the lump on my temple, where Kincaid's shoe had left its imprint. The night was miserably hot. Flares of light came and went as we passed street lights, filling stations, drive-ins.

I judged we were on Nebraska, headed away from town. The intervals between the light flares lengthened. Smith turned on a side street. When he turned again, the car jounced slightly. Wild palms and thickets crowded in. Smith slowed. The car weaved in the ruts of a sandy street.

Smith stopped the car and Kincaid said, "Get him out."

Smith did so, by taking hold of my collar and dragging me out. When he released me, my cheek fell against sand still hot from the sun. I drew my legs up, got my knees under me. Smith and Kincaid stood back and waited until I struggled to my feet.

I was standing in heavy shadows of palmetto and scrub pine. The harrumping of frogs came from not far away. I guessed we were in a swampy area not too far from Tina La Flor's cottage. The location might as well have been the moon.

"Now, Rivers," Kincaid said in the manner of a confident high school coach, "let's get with this thing. First, we're going to take the gag off and have a little talk. Okay? From there, it depends on you."

At a nod from Kincaid, Smith moved behind me and untied his handkerchief. He took it from my mouth and I spit. He used the handkerchief to wipe sweat off that pleasant, dumb face.

With a few of the cobwebs in my brains, I had the silly urge to tell him the truth: Look, mister, I don't know who you are or what you're after. Or what caused the most beautiful three-foot doll in the world to shinny over my transom. All I know is that I was minding my own business when a boat appeared one day and a chain reaction started. The circumstances surrounding the death of Bucks Jordan prohibit me from the police; so why don't you spend your time where it would do you more good?

I didn't say it, of course. As my head cleared, I faced up to the situation. The truth was a death warrant, now that they'd tipped their identity and connection with the unknown factors behind Bucks Jordan's murder. I'd live so long as they believed my living was worth something to them.

"Why don't you," Kincaid asked conversationally, "just tell us all about it?"

"Sure," Smith said, "we don't mean no real harm."

"With guns in your groceries?"

"It was you that started the fracas in the alley. The gun was just to be sure we talked to you."

"Kincaid," I said, "this guy's going to get you in serious

trouble one of these days. He's even dumber than you think."

"All right," Kincaid's tone cooled, "so we weren't balky at the thought of roughing you up, if necessary. On the other hand, we wanted to avoid it if we could. There's plenty to go around."

"Not the way Bucks told it," I said.

They exchanged a glance. Kincaid said, "Maybe he was holding out on you." He took a package of cigarettes from his jacket side pocket. He didn't light the cigarette but stood rolling it gently in his fingers until half the tobacco had dribbled out. "Or maybe you're thinking of holding out on us."

"Listen," Smith said, "we don't have to do business with this guy. Give me the blade you took off him and I'll save us some money."

The idea appealed to Kincaid. He stood thinking about it, and I did too—with the dismal frogs singing a dirge for me, a pale moon, remote and desolate, the single witness for me.

Sweat seeped down my arms and seemed to shrink the necktie binding my wrists.

"What do you want to know first?" I asked.

Kincaid nodded. "I'm glad to see that you recognize the odds are ten thousand to zero, in our favor, Rivers. Where is the little woman?"

"Tina?"

"Is there another?" he said impatiently.

"I don't know."

"Gimme the blade," Smith said.

"No, I think he's telling the truth. It's possible that he wouldn't know right at this moment. Are you to meet her later?"

"Yes."

"When?"

I licked my lips. "In a week."

"Fine. Now let's see if I have it straight. We never would have connected you with the little woman and Jordan, if she hadn't gone directly to you. We've learned in Ybor City that you've known her a considerable time. Did she ring you in early—or after she decided Jordan was too great a risk?"

"You're doing the summing up," I said. "Find out how bright you are."

"It doesn't matter when you entered the picture. Jordan's death meant a double-cross—and you're the only possible answer."

"You make me sound pretty rough," I said.

"You are pretty rough. And don't hand me a lot of malarkey about that private operator's license you carry. Even official cops take a chance, when the odds look right and stakes are high enough."

"Now we want the stakes," Smith said. "Pronto. No more gassing, understand? Kincaid, I'm tired of gassing."

"So am I. You heard the man, Rivers."

"I haven't got. . ." I broke off. Got what? What were the stakes?

"The little doll's got it?" Kincaid asked.

"I don't know."

"Look, friend," Smith said, "I'm going to carve you up unless . . ."

Kincaid cut him off with a gesture. Edging closer to me, Kincaid said, "You seem to have a dearth of knowledge to be in the middle of the thing, Rivers."

"It's the truth. But I'm not the only one in the middle. You keep me alive and kicking and I'll try to make a deal with Tina."

"Think you can?"

"Why not?"

"You don't seem to have done too well for yourself."

"I came in late," I said.

"After Bucks took Tina out to the *Sprite?*"

"Sure," I said, "after she met the Lessards."

Grope in the dark, you fall in the ditch. I felt myself go

in right then. I saw a sudden realization come to life in Kincaid's eyes. His face quickly went acid with anger.

"Why you. . ." he said in a choked tone. "You've let us think. . . . You're nothing but a strong-arm the little doll hired. You don't *know* where the stuff is!"

I didn't bother to ask how I'd slipped. I had an idea. Somehow, and for some reason, Bucks had taken Tina to the *Sprite* without anyone knowing it, until later. Until Kincaid and Smith had come ashore and started searching.

They didn't need me now.

Chapter Nine

As they closed in, I broke away momentarily, kicking at Smith and spinning from Kincaid's reaching hands. I plunged straight into the thicket, head down, not worrying about minor things such as brambles tearing at my eyeballs.

Tough, green, fibrous vegetation slashed my scalp. Muck sucked at my feet. Added to the sounds of quick motion behind me was Kincaid's voice, softly, "Okay, let's see how tough you are."

With my hands tied behind me, Smith was eager and happy, expressing his feelings with a short laugh. I broke out of the thicket, reaching a small wilderness of ankle deep water and lashing sawgrass. With civilization a few blocks away.

I glanced over my shoulder and saw them coming from different angles, making me the point in the triangle.

I dodged Smith's charge, water showering from my feet to make a brief lace of diamonds in the moonlight. Then Kincaid's weight hit me.

I stumbled, trying to shake him loose. Smith rammed his bulk against us: I went down, flat on my face, no hands to break my fall. Breath was crushed out of me. Swamp water shot into my nose to strangle me. My forehead came in contact with the black sand beneath the shallow water, and the sand was like a brick wall.

A period of time followed in which nothing was clear. My instincts were enraged at the indignity and desperately set against dying. A dream-like Smith hit me on the chin in a weird slow motion. I had the vague knowledge that I'd

62

struggled to my knees and that I'd keep getting up, again and again, until I'd worn the dirty son out.

Then I was floating along, with a numbness like a poisonous sleep stealing over me, as they carried me out of the muck.

Then sensation faded.

The sounds of a rasping effort to get breath were the next thing I heard. Sounds like a stricken heart patient makes when nothing is important except one more grain of oxygen. There was no heart patient—only me.

I was lathered in smothering sweat. Blood pounded through my temples. The gag was back in my mouth, but it was not the gag that made the effort to breath such a hard job. I was stuffed, cramped, in a very small space. I discovered this when I tried to move.

I bit down on the handkerchief against the pain lancing through my chest. The smell of my prison was compounded of fresh rubber and paint. Like the trunk of a car. And then I knew that's where I was, when I turned my head and felt the tread of a spare tire against my cheek.

Thoughts filtered through. New car. My car. Stuffed in the trunk of my car. Waterproof trunk . . . air proof.

I was blacking out again, dragging dead air through the handkerchief, air that had a another few seconds of life in it.

I felt the confines of the car trunk closing on me, the total darkness filling with a vibration like the beating of tiny wings.

I tried to scream. A crack on the skull brought a little sanity. I slumped, laboring for another breath. The beating wings retreated a few inches in the darkness.

I couldn't fight the panic any further back than the edges of my consciousness, but I managed to keep it there. I began working my wrists against the necktie bond. The tie was sodden, strong. My ears were ringing with the need for air.

The tie stretched a little, slipped on my sweat-slick wrist. I curled my thumb under and kept tugging. The tie hung on my knuckles. Then I barked my elbow on metal as my hand slid free.

My fingers were numb as they fumbled with the knot of the handkerchief. Big, dead sausages that were useless while angry needles bit deeper in my chest and invisible buzz saws worked on the joints of my twisted body.

The handkerchief knot gave. The rag fell away. I sucked in mouthfuls of the darkness, but pinpoints of light began to flare in my brain. My senses were slipping, my chest caving under an enormous weight as the process of suffocation neared its end.

I called feebly for help, or imagined that I did. My fingers groped in empty air. I was losing coordination, all sense of orientation.

My head rolled on my shoulders, coming to rest against the spare tire tread.

I thought of millions of tires on millions of cars, all rolling around through open country air, or the sweet smog of cities.

Tires filled with air . . .

My groping fingers found direction. A valve cap. It turned.

Teeth set against the pain of the contortions, I worked my face close to the valve cap of the spare tire. My fingernail slipped off the slight protrusion of the valve stem. Then I had the stem centered. I pressed. Air hissed—and for a second I was too choked up to take full advantage of it.

I used the air in short bursts until the sizzling cooled in my lungs and the ringing eased in my ears. I developed a terrific headache, but I accepted it as a gratifying symptom. Dead heads don't hurt.

With death a tire's worth of air away, my fingers searched the steel prison. Besides me and the spare, the trunk held a bumper jack and lug wrench. Laboriously, between gulps of air, I worked the jack handle from its position behind the spare. It was flattened at one end.

I located the trunk catch with my fingers and inserted the flat end of the jack handle. The trunk creaked as I pried. I kept at it, resting, getting a squirt of air, levering at the latch.

The latch weakened. When it snapped, it surrendered almost effortlessly.

The handle slipped from my fingers. I crawled over the rim of the trunk and fell on the ground.

I was too weak to get up. I rolled to my back and took a fresh look at open sky while I dragged breath deep in my lungs. The moon was gone. A deep, pre-dawn hush lay over the earth. A few tendrils of mist writhed off the swampy water beyond the unused, sandy back street.

I reached for the bumper, pulled myself up, finally got my feet under me. I hung on against the blinding pain in my head and the tired, hard beating of my heart.

The TV cowboys can take a dozen punches to the chin and wreck a saloon without mussing their hair. Not me.

For the time being, I'd had it.

I woke in early afternoon, the sweat-soaked daybed in my apartment as comfortable as a pot of lumpy, hot paste. My eyes were swollen from hard, exhausted sleep. Stiff and sore, I bit back a groan as I swung to a sitting position on the edge of the bed.

I pushed myself upright, padded to the bathroom, and started cold water in the tub. I toweled off some of the sweat from my face, neck, brown mat of chest, draped the towel across my naked shoulder and headed for the kitchenette.

While I waited for coffee to perk, I sat down at the kitchenette table, opened a cold pint of beer and tried to get my thoughts in order.

Memory of the drive home was vague. I'd used the spare key wired under the hood to put the car in service. I'd crawled up to the apartment, swallowed three headache pills, stripped to my shorts, and fallen on the bed.

For awhile I'd died. The rest of the world hadn't. People like Kincaid and Smith had been out and doing. The beer tasted like poison at the thought of that pair.

They'd told me more than is told to a man who is expected to live. They'd intended for me to die, after they got what they wanted.

Score one. Score one where it will never be forgotten.

They'd told me that an Item had been aboard the *Sprite.* Bucks Jordan had taken Tina La Flor out to the schooner. The Item had disappeared.

Following this disappearance, Bucks had been hell-set on getting his hands on Tina. Instead, he had got himself killed.

It seemed reasonable that the *Sprite,* once the Item was recovered, would go as she had come, into the vastness of the sea. With her would go my chance of proving to the Tampa police that I had not beat Bucks Jordan to death.

I had no way of knowing how many hours were left to me. Kincaid and Smith were diligent, and Kincaid was smart.

On my other flank was Lieutenant Steve Ivey. You don't staff a cosmopolitan city with dumb country sheriffs who are wise only in the realm of dirty, crooked politics. You use scientists in the labs and put men in the unmarked cars who have FBI Academy training in their background. It was a simple question of time until that kind of organization linked me with Bucks Jordan.

And maybe a shorter time before the *Sprite* started her auxiliaries to take her to deep water where she'd belly her sails.

Thumbnail the next two hours: I dunked in cold water, braced with coffee, Cuban sausage and eggs. Wiped up an old gun, my spare. Made a mental note to go by the office for the duplicate set of keys and have that set duplicated.

Killed a second pint of icy beer while I made with the telephone.

I wanted a lead on Tina, and I wanted it bad. She could identify the Item—and it was the Item that was worth murder.

I talked with personages white, tan and black. People who knew where the skeletons were closeted.

I got a result, in a negative way. Tina had pulled it off.

She was unbelievably well hidden. Or far away from Tampa. Or dead.

When I got over to the ramshackle frame house and knocked on the door, little Miguel Cardezas told me that ma-ma was in the backyard.

I went around the house. A flop-eared stray dog regarded me from the cool underside, scratched his ribs against one of the concrete block pillars on which the house stood, and tagged behind me.

Mrs. Cardezas was anchored in a cane-bottomed chair in the middle of the small, bare yard. The sun shone on the jet coils of her hair. The chair creaked under the weight of her ample body as she bent forward to dip a chicken in a small tub of hot water on the ground before her. She withdrew the headless fowl, and feathers started vanishing from the carcass.

"Good afternoon," I said.

She paused in her chicken-picking, brushed a wisp of hair from her forehead with the back of her hand, careful not to transfer any of the small feathers sticking to her hand.

"Como esta?"

"Not so good."

"You've been ill?" She looked up at me with concern. Her round, generous face was misty with fine perspiration.

"I nearly got killed," I said, "fighting Tina La Flor's fight."

"Oh, Señor Rivers . . ."

"Never mind that," I said. "Think about Tina."

"Si."

"Do you know where she is?"

Her hand moved. I had the feeling that she was about to cross herself. "No, señor."

"Mrs. Cardezas . . ."

She stood up, imploring with her hands before her, the dangling chicken detracting none from her expression. "Señor Rivers, I asked you to help Tina. Now I am sorry. I don't want you harmed. Neither would she. Get out of it, señor.

Forget that you know of it. It will work out, and she will be safe."

The happy hound whipped my leg with his wagging tail. "It isn't that simple, Mrs. Cardezas."

"Don't be unwise, señor! There are others . . ." She broke off.

"Others? Who?"

"I ask you . . ."

"Who, Mrs. Cardezas?"

"He was concerned for her also, the little fellow who called himself Gaspar."

"Little fellow?"

"A dwarf, señor. A most sympathetic little man with bowed legs."

"When was he here?"

"Señor . . . please . . ."

"Today?"

"*Si.* Yes," she sighed. "This morning. But he saw the folly of increasing the danger to Tina."

I caught the implication in her tone, the accusation in the large, dark eyes. "You think that I'm increasing the danger to her?"

"Now I do," she stated. "If you are being watched, followed, and you should find her . . ."

"I'm going to find her, Mrs. Cardezas."

I turned and started away. She followed me to the corner of the house, calling my name once. I glanced back when I reached the sidewalk. She was standing in the narrow driveway, the chicken in her hand. Both she and the chicken looked tired and wilted from the heat.

Gaspar the Great was an Ybor City character. I didn't think I'd have much trouble finding him.

I started the rounds with a two-fold request, talking with bartenders, restaurant operators, hackies at their stands, characters in back rooms who had an aversion to daylight.

First I said, Rivers wants two newcomers to the local scene named Kincaid and Smith.

Second I said, where is Gaspar the Great?

Two hours and thirty minutes later I walked into a neighborhood tavern. There were two male customers down the bar talking quietly. The bartender was a supple man of Spanish descent in his mid-forties. He had a patrician face, high forehead, thin nose and likewise a patrician bearing.

"Hi, Ed." His voice was much more democratic than his looks.

I let him have the first question, adding the description of the pair that I was scattering all over Ybor City.

He shook his head. "Don't know them."

"Keep an eye out?"

"Sure."

"Seen Gaspar the Great recently?"

The bartender jerked a thumb toward the back of the place. "I believe he's in the gentleman's lounge."

I walked down the bar. The tavern's rear area was a long ell adjacent to the bar. A television set, tuned to a regatta across the bay at St. Petersburg, was mounted on a high shelf facing the length of the room.

On one of the round tables were a cluttered ashtray, a half-full glass of beer, and small, moisture-beaded pitcher with an inch of beer left at the bottom.

I helped myself to a chair at the table and watched the televising of the roaring hydroplanes trying to tear themselves free of the water.

I heard the scrape of small footsteps, and turned the chair.

On his bowed legs, Gaspar rolled his way to the table. He was no midget. He was a dwarf, with arms, legs and lower torso that had failed to mature. His head, face and upper torso were of normal size. Misshapen as he was, he had the agility of a monkey, and something of the monkey in the appearance of his face, which was swarthy and deeply wrinkled. He had dark, bushy hair that grew low on his forehead.

He reached up to grasp the back of the chair and edge of the table. He seemed to bounce from the floor to the chair. He sat on the edge of the table and smiled a greeting at me.

"Long time no see, Ed."

"How've things been?"

He shrugged, made a vague gesture toward his clothing. He was wearing a tropical weight that had cost him plenty, but he'd paid that bill a long time ago. Neatly pressed, the suit showed its age in its high shine and threadbare edges.

I'd heard that in the old days Gaspar the Great had gone in for silk shirts, shoes by an English shoemaker. He'd headlined, with two other dwarfs, a trapeze act that had earned fabulous amounts. He'd carried a personal valet with him and had a penchant for walking into a place and buying champagne for the house.

But there was gray in his mop of wiry, unruly hair now, and the decline of the carny and circus circuits was old, bitter history.

Chapter Ten

He drained the contents of the beer pitcher into his glass. "Join me, Ed?"

"If I can buy."

"Why not?" he said with a grim edge in his voice.

I ordered the beer. He gestured a silent toast and said, "I got a feeling you came in here looking for me."

"That's right. Did you find Tina La Flor?"

"Who said I was looking for her? Oh—I know. Mrs. Cardezas."

I nodded.

"Well, I didn't find her," he said. "In fact, I quit looking. I can't help her out of the kind of trouble she's in now. The cops'll find her soon enough, is my guess. What's your angle, Ed?"

"I have a client."

"Who wants you to find Tina?" His brows quirked haughtily. "You expect me to sell out the little doll? I am assuredly money hungry. I would put my mother's navel on display for money. But to sell out . . ."

"Take it easy," I said. "I'm not necessarily against her."

"No?" His dark eyes, set in muddy yellow whites, were cautious. "Who is this client?"

"Maybe a guy on a boat."

"Boat? What boat?"

"Mean anything to you?"

"Can't say that it does."

"You have no idea where Tina is?"

He shook his head. He seemed to have something on his mind. "What is this about a boat, Ed?"

"If it means nothing . . ."

"Damn it," he said angrily, his normally guttural voice piping slightly, "it doesn't, in itself. But Tina's an old friend. We little people got to stick together. If somebody's carried her off on a boat, I want something done about it."

"They haven't, I don't think," I said.

I let him simmer down. Then I said, "I'm also looking for a couple guys. Named Kincaid and Smith. Strangers. Bumped into them?"

"Kincaid and Smith?" He measured his beer with his eyes. "No, haven't heard of them."

"I want them," I said. "Bad."

He shuddered faintly. "I'd hate to be in their shoes."

I left him morosely staring into his beer.

The afternoon was nearly gone. From a drugstore phone booth, I checked the telephone answering service.

A woman who gave her name as Mrs. Maria Scanlon had tried three times to reach me that afternoon.

I hung up and stood thinking about that for a few seconds. I dropped a dime in the phone and dialed information. No phone was listed at the address of the Scanlons' cottage, at least not in their name.

I had to fight rush hour traffic crosstown. I saw no sign of life at the Scanlon cottage when I approached it.

I parked the car, got out, and crossed the sandy yard. The cottage was typical of those jerry-built cracker boxes erected in Florida twenty to thirty years ago. There were five or six rooms enclosed in un-insulated pine siding, with the inevitable screened porch of that era strung along the front. It was graceless, unattractive.

I rattled the screen door. The cottage showed no sign of life. As I was about to turn away, I heard someone inside.

Maria Scanlon appeared on the porch. Her stocky, bovine figure was clothed in a wrinkled, soiled print dress. The drab brown hair bunned at the back of her flat-faced head spilled wisps about her ears and neck.

"Rivers . . . I've been trying to reach you."

"I got the message."

"Please come in."

I followed her into a cramped living room. She was one hell of a housekeeper. Ashtrays were full all over the place. Old papers and magazines were stacked in a corner. Propped over that junk was a tangle of cheap fishing gear, burma poles dripping carelessly loose line. On a small table the remains of sandwiches were drawing a swarm of gnats.

I took the chair she indicated. She seated herself on the nearby couch, knees close together, back straight.

Hands folded in her lap, she studied me closely. Her eyes held a hint of an avid, unnerving quality.

"May I call you Ed?"

"Sure."

"I— Would you like a drink?"

"No, thanks."

"Do you mind if I`. . ."

"Go right ahead."

She jumped up, hurried through the plastered archway to the dining room. On the buffet were a couple of bottles and a dirty glass or two. She shook the dregs from one glass into another and poured herself a drink of a heavy-bodied brandy.

She returned to the living room, sat down, and sipped the brandy. "I haven't been sleeping well. I— A little brandy helps one to relax, don't you think?"

I waited.

"Mr. Rivers . . . Ed . . . I've been upset about our last meeting. You seemed suspicious of me. You seemed to think that an object of some kind had disappeared from the *Sprite* and that I knew what it was. I don't know anything about the *Sprite*, really. I had to explain that."

"Why?"

"Because I don't want you feeling suspicious of me. There is—I want you to do something for me." She killed the brandy. "You're a private detective, and I want to retain you for a job. I can't do that if you think all manner of wrong things about me, can I?

"So far as the schooner is concerned, I never saw the boat or the people who own her until Jack introduced us."

"Where'd he meet them?"

"I think it was somewhere in Latin America, a long while before I met him. One day he told me that the Lessards were cruising here. We would meet them, have a vacation. So we left New Orleans and came here." She studied the glass, then raised her eyes to me. "Did you find what you were looking for?"

"Not yet."

"Kincaid and Smith?"

"I met them. We had a talk."

She looked toward the brandy, but she didn't get up. "Is Jack in trouble, Ed?"

"I don't know. Is he?"

Her underlip curled over her teeth. She bit down slightly. After a little, she said, "Alex and D. D.—I understand them. Alex is a man of many frustrations. Nothing he has ever done turned out quite right. He's one of those people who're always off balance in the world, and he seethes with the continuous effort to get in the rhythm of living." Her eyes drifted toward the empty window, the darkening sky beyond. "There are so many like him . . ."

"And D. D.?"

"She lives in a lonely world of icebergs." Maria Scanlon's brows quirked. Briefly, she was pleased with herself. It was my guess that she was telling herself that her remark had been dreadfully astute, one she must remember. "D. D.'s moral lapses are made consciously, Ed. The efforts of a person striking at the emptiness of her life."

"You seem to know a lot about the Lessards," I said, "to have just met them."

"I don't need to be around people forever to sum them up," she said quietly.

"Then the loose way the Lessards seem to live is not their fault?"

"Oh, no. There's a spark of brilliance in both Alex and his daughter. If society had provided the right conditions, their talents would have borne fruit."

She enjoyed clichés. I wondered how many textbooks she had read.

I leaned toward her. "But you're afraid of them."

"No. . . ."

"Not for yourself. For Jack, maybe."

She didn't answer that.

"Jack has been behaving quite well," she said finally. "But if something has disappeared from the *Sprite* . . ."

"You're afraid they'll think Jack took it."

"Not the Lessards."

"Kincaid and Smith?"

"I don't know. I just don't know." She folded her arms and hugged herself. Her heavy bosom squeezed up like overly heavy twin udders. She got up, obeying the call of the brandy bottle.

I waited.

She gave the brandy bottle a heavier tap. I wondered how much of that stuff she could take in without showing it. Probably more than most men.

"Kincaid and Smith been around?" I asked.

"Yes. Several times. I thought nothing of it. After all, they were Alex Lessard's employees. But in the light of what you said when we last met . . . I really have worried about it."

"They've got Jack into something?"

She looked at me levelly. "Not yet. I'm sure of it. But if they sneaked something aboard that boat and have lost it . . . Jack's inclined toward what he calls deals. They attract

him. Of course it's because he knew such poverty in early
life. He was ambitious. He wanted decent things, like everybody else. They were denied him, and he developed this . . .
this urge to take shortcuts."

"You think Kincaid and Smith might ring your husband
in?"

"If they need help—and I can't let that happen."

"What can you do?" I asked.

"Keep circumstances in proper arrangement."

"That's a pretty tall order, Mrs. Scanlon. Even some good
statesmen have tried."

"But my area is smaller. One man. Not a state or a nation.
I—I know what is needed."

"What is that?"

"Money."

The word brought a short silence.

I began to suspect the bait with which she'd hooked Scanlon. "How much did you have?"

"I—my parents—they didn't understand. They cut me off
when I married Jack, the narrow-minded . . . I wish they
were dead!" She wiped the corner of her mouth with the back
of her hand. "I had a few thousand, my own. An inheritance
from a grandparent, my maternal grandmother."

"It's gone?"

She eased to the edge of the couch. "Almost, but I can get
more."

"That's where I come in? The job you wanted done?"

She nodded. "My grandmother's jewelry is in a safety
deposit box in a New Orleans bank. As a private detective
you're bonded, aren't you?"

I nodded.

"Then it's simple," she said. "You'll go to New Orleans and
bring the jewels to me."

Chapter Eleven

A look of relief had spread over her face. It died by slow degrees, as she read meaning in my silence.

"You mean you won't do it?" she asked in disbelief.

"That's right."

"But—you're a detective. For hire. You must go."

"I don't must anything, lady."

"Listen, I've depended on this!" Her plain face began to grow ugly.

"There are other ways of getting the jewels."

"No!"

"Go yourself," I said.

"And leave Jack here alone?" She was stunned, then angry. The ugliness spread.

"Take him with you."

"And have him find out. . . ." she bit the words off.

"How much there is?" I finished for her. "If he knew, he'd take it all in one grab, right?"

"That's none of your business," she said, controlling herself, remembering that she needed me. "Why won't you go?"

"I'm busy here," I said.

I stood up. She rose also. She grabbed my arm. "You don't like me!" she cried, her voice shrilling to a selfish peak.

Her face was sweaty and flushed. For a second I glimpsed an ugly brat, ugly inside as well as out, a slimy little stinker spoiled rotten by parents attempting to fill the gaps in her life, gaps made by her own appearance and personality.

In defeat, her parents had finally let her go with Scanlon

and disowned her, perhaps hoping it would bring her to her senses. She might as well get it through her head that the rest of the world wasn't going to be as long-suffering as parents.

I jerked free of her. The rebuff outraged her. With a dirty word in her mouth, she tried to scratch my face.

I shoved her back on the couch. She flopped like a sack of sand and lay with her eyes burning on me. She was gasping for breath. Sweat clustered in heavy drops on her forehead.

"Damn you," she whispered. "You're cruel and evil. I tried to understand you. And now I do. You killed Bucks Jordan. I'll tell the police. . . ."

I bent over her and said, "You tell the police one single lie and I'll break your fat, stupid neck."

She cowered away, as if she would go crawling over the end of the couch like a creeping slug.

I straightened. And saw Jack Scanlon standing in the doorway.

I wondered how much he'd heard and seen and what interpretation he would give it. I didn't move, and neither did he for about a full minute. Maria got off the couch as if she were barefoot and stepping on broken glass.

"Jack . . ." she said.

"Save it," he said. Rays of the sinking sun streamed across the screened porch to limn his rangy, rawboned tallness and to glint on his black hair. The result was to put the rugged, lazy, lean features of his face in shadows.

"Seems like every time I see you, Rivers," he said, "you're talking to my wife." He moved into the room. His eyes moved lazily between Maria and me. "How about that?" he laughed without humor. "Big ugly man; dumpy, ugly woman. Just a couple of lonely souls trying to cheer each other up. Well, what about that! Maria, I didn't know you had it in you."

She moved toward him cautiously. "Jack, it isn't . . ."

"Rivers," he said, ignoring her pointedly, "if the heifer's in heat, don't mind me."

"Oh, God, Jack!" she cried in such ragged agony that I couldn't help feeling sorry for her.

"Big man," Scanlon continued to scathe me. "Big private cop. Why don't you act big, big man?"

"Jack . . ." Her face was streaming moisture now, partly sweat, partly tears.

He shoved her away from him.

"It's my house, big man. Move, that's all. Just flick a muscle at me. I'll gut-shoot you, big man. Then call the cops. Like that. Tell them I caught a man in my house, with my wife. Maria'll tell them exactly what I say for her to tell them, all the things you bust in here and done to her."

Maria was standing tight against the wall where he'd pushed her. She turned her wet face toward me.

"Please leave," she said hoarsely.

"I didn't tell him to leave yet," Scanlon said. He was enjoying himself, hugely, twistedly. In him, pleasure had taken the form of a perversion.

"Ain't every day a man walks in and finds his wife with a big, ugly man," he went on. He dropped a glance at her. "One thing, Rivers, you sure as hell must be hard up."

I began to tremble with the effort to control myself. I started for the door. He moved toward me.

"Did I say you could leave, big man?"

Somebody should have told him better. He mistook the whiteness of my face. He was too sure of himself, and it gave me all the advantage.

When he reached for me, a grin on his face, I snapped his arm up, spun him, grabbed a handful of that black hair, and threw him flat on the floor.

He lay dazed, the wind knocked out of him.

"I ought to kick your teeth in," I said.

Maria caught my arm, throwing her weight against me.

The suddenness of it sent me staggering a few feet from Scanlon.

"Don't you touch him!" she said viciously.

I pushed her back. She stayed between Scanlon and me.

"It appeared to him," she said, "that he'd walked in on a man roughing up his wife. An eruption took place inside of him."

"Sure," I said sarcastically.

"Don't you use that tone! Whatever Jack said to me was spoken in heat."

"Of the eruption," I said.

Scanlon got to his feet behind her, his eyes hating me, his face no longer pleasant. Unpleasant for keeps, so far as I was concerned.

He touched her shoulder. "It's all right, Maria."

"No, it isn't. I won't have anyone throwing you down and threatening to kick you . . ."

"I said it's all right!"

She pouted, but kept her mouth shut. The pressure of his hand on her shoulder forced her to one side.

"Okay, Rivers, what's it all about?"

I caught the glint of despair in her eyes as she suspected I was going to mention the last of her resources lying in a New Orleans strongbox.

With a heavy, mechanical motion, she moved to the couch and dropped on its edge in a slumped, sitting position.

"I'm still looking for Kincaid and Smith," I said.

"You expect to find them here?"

"I thought she might tell me something about them. More correctly, I thought you might, but you weren't here when I came."

Her head turned as she ventured a glance at me.

"She don't know them."

"You do?"

He shrugged. "No more than you—or her. They worked the boat. Alex introduced us. They got off the boat."

"You never saw them before they came here?"

"No."

"Where are they staying?"

"How should I know?" He shrugged.

"Why'd you come here?"

"You go to hell, Rivers."

"I've ways of finding out."

"Go ahead and use your ways. I got nothing to hide— except of course thirty-three dead men buried under the house. Go right ahead and dig them up."

"You met Alex Lessard in Latin America," I said.

"Well, you got to meet your future friends someplace."

"You were kicked out of one of the countries down there after a revolution misfired."

His lips grinned. His eyes didn't. "I see you've already been using your ways. So what if I was? That's in the past. I'm a respectable man now, complete with wife."

"Was Lessard in the same deal?"

He threw back his head and laughed. "You got a good imagination. Lessard was wildcatting for oil when I met him. It didn't pan out. He lost his own shirt, plus the pants of a couple of backers. Being two Americans in the same neck of the woods, we got to be friends, even if our interests was different."

"Just a couple of Boy Scouts camping in a strange woods," I said.

"Now look, Rivers . . . ah, the hell with you. When Alex planned this trip, he got in touch. If he was going to be in the States, I wanted to see him. I got a right, ain't I? To see an old friend? So Maria and I came here to meet the boat."

"No longer Boy Scouts," I said. "Now you're some tired tourists basking in the Florida sun."

His eyes darkened. Then he lifted his shoulders in that quick shrug. "You can't bait me, Rivers. You got it all now, wrapped up and complete."

"Okay," I said. "But take one bit of advice."

"For free?"

"No charge whatever. Don't be in a hurry to leave Tampa."

"Says who?"

"Me."

"Yeah? For how long?"

"Until I tell you that you can leave."

He watched me stonily as I walked out of the cottage.

From the Scanlon cottage, I drove the short distance to the bait camp. The lean, sun-cured proprietor helped a middle-aged tourist couple out of a boat they'd brought in from an afternoon of fishing. The man was a pudgy cigar smoker who looked slightly ridiculous in a Hawaiian shirt and Bermudas. His rotund little wife wore a coolie hat and sun glasses along with her cotton dress and straw guaraches. They chatted about their afternoon of fishing. I supposed they'd return to some little town where she'd recount her experiences to the Thursday Literary Club.

The pompous little man, with condescending gestures, told the bait camp owner he could have the afternoon's catch. Half a dozen grunts—trash fish to the natives.

The couple wended their way under the pines to a block-long Caddy. The proprietor lifted the kicker from the dinghy, carried it down the pier, and grunted it into a steel drum of fresh water, attaching the motor to the rim of the drum. He'd start it and rinse the salty impurities of sea water from it.

"How-do," he said. "Have some grunts."

"Thanks, but I'm not that hungry."

"*Turistas,*" he said. Then he spat, in the manner of the Latins.

"I'm still looking for a couple of *turistas,*" I said.

"Kincaid and Smith?"

"Right."

"They ain't been back since you was here."

"Who's out there now?" I nodded toward the *Sprite* riding at anchor on the glassy smooth water.

"I dunno. Lessard and his gal young-un, I think. Want a flat-bottom?"

I fished the rental from my wallet.

"Take your pick," he said. "Snug her when you get back. I'm going to eat my supper."

Alex Lessard spotted me rowing out and stood at the fore-deck rail, a spindly figure until I got close to him. Then the intensity of his face, his stance, was apparent, and the spindliness became wiry strength. His narrow face was unhappy, his brooding gray eyes cold. The last red rays of the sun gave the naked top of his narrow skull a gnarled, seasoned-walnut appearance.

He wore the faded khaki trunks and sneakers that seemed to be his usual attire when he was aboard.

I tied the flat-bottom to the ladder and secured the oars. When I raised up and looked at him, I sensed a decision in his bitter eyes.

"Welcome aboard, Rivers," he said quietly. "You're in time for dinner."

He offered me a hand up, stood aside for me. In white formal attire, he would have been as much at home at a dinner in a South American embassy.

Courteously, he motioned me aft. I wasn't fooled. I was as welcome here as a leak in the auxiliary engine's gas tanks.

At the sound of our footsteps, D. D. came on deck. She stopped abruptly when she saw me. She was a dream in shorts and halter, her short ash blonde hair in slight curls misted to her temples and forehead.

She appeared to be cold sober, her eyes hollow, her face touched with paleness from her last prolonged bout with the jug.

"Mr. Rivers is having dinner with us, D. D. Unless you've dined already, Mr. Rivers?"

"No," I told Lessard, "I haven't."

"We're having pre-packaged TV dinners," D. D. said. "I'll slip one out of the refrigerator and into the oven for you."

She disappeared into the cabin. On the afterdeck under a collapsible awning a small folding table and chairs had been set up. Lessard continued his role of graceful host.

"Please sit down, Mr. Rivers." Would I care for a cigarette. A martini. He stirred vermouth and gin in a chipped crockery pitcher with all the aplomb of a duke presiding over a cut crystal cocktail service.

I decided to play it his way. We had dinner while the sky darkened and a light breeze came out of the Gulf to ripple the awning.

On the surface, it was almost romantic. A schooner that had been everywhere. Two men and a beautiful woman enjoying the last moments of a lazy tropical day. A passing boat might have envied us.

D. D. was quick to smile, quick-witted and charming. Alex Lessard didn't for a moment fail to keep the pretense going that I was a welcome guest.

He was interesting as a conversationalist. He had been far, seen much. Under the cynical exterior was a keen mind that feared nothing. Maybe his view of life was too big, too complete, so broad that an individual's living or dying was of no real importance.

Probably his failures had, brick by brick, built his attitude. When life itself is sufficiently reduced in importance, failures here and there mean nothing.

Talking with him gave me a growing certainty of one thing. I'd faced plenty of tough ones in my time, all the way from hoodlums to an old lady who'd kill mercilessly to keep family scandals secret, to a ravening madman who wanted to soak the pain out of his head with my blood. None of them had been any more dangerous than Alex Lessard.

Chapter Twelve

Dinner over, D. D. cleared the table and brought a bottle of brandy and two glasses from the galley.

"I think I'll have a swim," she said. "Join me, Ed?"

"I doubt that Mr. Rivers came here to swim," Lessard said.

D. D. went into the cabin. Lessard poured brandy. D. D. came out, her bathing suit and hair bold splashes of white in the early darkness. She went forward with a wave of her hand. A few seconds later, the sound of her plunge in the water came to us.

The Gulf breeze spared Lessard the bother of squirting insect repellent. Even in sitting, he was in an attitude of intensity. He listened to the forward splash. "When she was a small girl, her mother always warned her not to swim until an hour after she'd eaten," he said.

"Her mother must have been a beautiful woman."

"Yes," Lessard said, hissing the "s" heavily. Light flared over the chiseled sharpness of his features as he lighted a cigarette. "Shall we get down to business, Rivers?"

"Why not?"

"You're still looking for Kincaid and Smith."

"Right."

"I wish you'd update me," he said. "I honestly don't know what's going on." His cigarette coal arced bright as he threw up his hands. "First you come out here looking for Bucks Jordan. Someone kills him. Then you reappear to question my daughter. Sounds quite serious."

"No picnic. Not for Bucks."

He was thoughtful for a moment. "D. D. was not too drunk to remember the details of your visit."

"I really came out to see you."

"Sorry I missed you. But thanks for going in after her when she fell overboard. She—usually she isn't so quickly cooled off when she goes on a . . . well, rampage. Perhaps the fault is mine. I haven't lived the sort of life conducive to the proper rearing of a daughter. But you surely can't believe she had anything serious to do with a man like Bucks Jordan."

"I'm trying to find out."

"Someone has been telling you tales out of school. If D. D. flirted a trifle with him, it was out of boredom. And because he was such an asinine fool. Believe me, we hardly knew the man. I've explained all that. Now I think you owe me an explanation or two."

"Fire away."

"Why do you keep coming here?"

"I'm working."

"Who is your client?"

"You got a good technique," I said. "You fire your questions."

"You think Jordan's death has some connection with this boat, don't you?"

"To be honest, yes."

"Then go to the police."

"I'll work in my own way, Lessard."

"Perhaps I'll go to them myself."

"And tell them what?"

"That I put into this port with the proper clearance. That Jordan worked for me briefly and quit. That I never saw him before I came to Tampa and know nothing about him. That you will not believe the truth but persist in improper invasion of privacy."

The velvet gloves were coming off now. He leaned forward. "In appearance, you're not above suspicion yourself, Rivers. You're no fresh-faced schoolboy in a clean Peter Pan collar."

"Meaning?"

"I'm beginning to take you seriously," he said. It was softly spoken, but it was a warning and a threat. "I'm wondering what you're up to, why you haven't gone to the police. I've heard of private detectives who are not above blackmail and extortion."

"I'm not one of those," I said.

"You act like it. You act as if you're trying to build suspicion against us while keeping it secret from the police. If you hope to scare us into paying you money simply because a man now deceased worked on this boat . . ."

"It isn't only Jordan."

"No?"

"There are Kincaid and Smith."

"I don't follow you."

"Maybe you do, and maybe you don't," I said. "For now, I'll give you benefit of the doubt."

He jumped to his feet, his body quivering. "What a presumption—that you have the right to judge me!"

"Temper, father," D. D. said. She'd come aboard without our hearing. She stood beside the cabin, her body gleaming wetly in the near darkness.

"Go and swim some more," Lessard said angrily.

"I'd prefer a drink. This staying sober is for the birds." She raised her arms. Her body writhed in a stretch. She came sauntering toward me. "Ed, it's been a deadly dull day. I'd like a night on the mainland. What are you doing tonight?"

"D. D.!" Lessard practically screamed. The harried look of him intensified.

She laughed, flicked his chin with her forefinger, and strolled into the cabin.

"Maybe I'll take her up on the proposition," I said.

For a second I thought Lessard was going to hit me.

"She might be a more reasonable talker than her old man," I said.

"Reasonable? I've told you everything. Willingly. Honestly."

"You've told me nothing," I said, "that isn't designed to hide the truth."

I stood up. We faced each other.

"Listen, Lessard, Kincaid and Smith right now are hunting whatever it was that was taken from this boat. Bucks Jordan was killed after the theft was made. It all ties together. You brought something in here you shouldn't have. It disappeared, and hell broke loose."

He chain-lit a cigarette from his previous one. "So that's how you think it is?"

"That's the way it looks."

"Oh, hell," D. D. said from the cabin doorway, "tell him the truth, Alex. He's not going to rest until you do."

"D. D.," he said thinly, "I'd very much appreciate your staying . . ."

She came toward us with a drink in her hand. "He doesn't want to violate a confidence, Ed. And he has a thorough dislike," her eyes cut to her father, "for the authorities. Past experiences, y'know."

Their gazes held. Then Lessard jerked around, turning his back on her. He moved to the rail and stared in remote silence at the open water.

D. D. raised her hand and rubbed the stubble on my cheek with her open palm. She stood with her body loosely arched toward me.

"Like a little drinkee, Ed?"

"D. D. . . . ." Lessard half groaned in exasperation, his back remaining toward us.

"Yeah," I said, "of some of this truth that's about to spill all over the place."

"Oh, that. Well, Kincaid and Smith were not mere deckhands at all."

"Really."

"Don't sneer, darling. It doesn't become you." She tipped her glass and took a swallow. "We were berthed in Callao, opening our last can of beans when Kincaid and Smith ap-

proached us. They showed us their papers. They were American citizens. They wanted to get back to the States."

"Private-like," I said.

"You mean, there are airplanes and regular boats running?"

"I mean something like that."

"And why didn't they take one of them?" she asked with
a laugh. "You know, it didn't occur to us to ask them. When
you slip the can opener in those final beans it rather cuts
the bonds of being choosy."

"They must have made some explanation," I said. "You
don't risk yourself, a considerable length of time, and a
schooner such as this one blindly."

"They gave us a very believable explanation—voluntarily.
They'd had some trouble, they said, and were not able to leave
the country by the regular routes and modes.

"They offered to provision the *Sprite,* work their watches,
and give us a thousand dollars in cash when we dropped
anchor in Tampa.

"Alex and I saw it as a stroke of luck. We'd been wanting
to get out of there ourselves, and back to where folks spoke
English.

"We accepted their offer. They sneaked aboard at night,
bringing a couple of foot lockers of personal belongings.

"We put out of Callao with scanty supplies, ostensibly for
a couple of days fishing. We made port twice, further north,
and finished provisioning. Then a jolly ride until the towers
of Tampa appeared on the horizon. Kincaid and Smith gave
us our money and everybody was happy."

"Except Bucks Jordan."

"That," D. D. said, "is not in our bailiwick."

"Why were they coming here? Why, specifically, Tampa?"

"How would I know?"

"You had a lot of days on deck with them, long, lazy days.
Good talking days."

"They didn't talk much."

"Not even to you?"

"Well," she laughed, "I wasn't interested in their life history. Nor in their business. Kincaid mentioned once that he had relatives in Jacksonville. Tampa seemed a convenient spot for them to catch a plane and fly to Jax. Save us the long haul around the Florida peninsula, taking the canal and coming up the eastern shore of Mexico as we did."

"I hope no aged, starving grandmother is waiting for them in Jacksonville," I said.

"Don't you believe me, Ed?"

I honestly didn't know. She made it sound like the absolute truth—but that didn't rule out its being a complete pack of lies. She was capable of either.

"What were they carrying?"

"Two foot lockers," she said. "We didn't X-ray them or do a customs inspection."

She stood there regarding me coolly. "That's it, Ed. Buy it or junk it. We don't feel we've done anything wrong. But we did help them leave under questionable circumstances."

"If you really want to find Kincaid and Smith," Lessard said, turning from the rail, "try Jacksonville."

"On your say-so?"

"Don't be such a bear, Ed," D. D. said. "I'd go with you. You could keep your eye on me every minute."

Sure, I thought, until Lessard had time to do whatever was necessary here.

The thought must have reflected on my face.

"My, my," D. D. said, "aren't we suspicious!"

"I'll think it over," I told her. "Thanks for the dinner, Lessard."

I went forward, climbing over the side, and began manhandling the flat-bottom toward the lights on shore.

I heard the sound of her cleave the water. She came up a few feet from the flat-bottom, her face and hair a white sculptured image rising out of the dark water.

Playfully, she splashed water toward me. The shower of

drops lived with a brief phosphorescent glow. A few of them reached me, falling warmly on my face and chest.

"Think quickly, Ed," she called softly. "Jax would be a lot of fun."

Then she treaded water as the flat-bottom moved away from her.

I went home, stripped to my waist, toweled the sweat off my chest, and opened a can of beer. It was so cold it hurt my teeth.

I called Western Union and sent a telegram to New Orleans. It requested the agency man there to find out if any New Orleans bank had a safety deposit box registered to Maria Blake, or Maria Blake Scanlon, or Maria Scanlon. If she had a box, I'd assume it wasn't empty, but held the jewels, as she'd said.

I didn't feel easy about the telegram, and wouldn't have sent it if I could have avoided it. I wasn't worried about difficulties the New Orleans office might encounter. I knew I'd get the information.

It was the thought of the Home Office that had me bugged. Routine reports from New Orleans were going to raise the question as to what I was doing in Tampa, what was going on here.

If I got out of this thing, I'd have an explanation the Home Office would understand and accept. If not, an explanation wouldn't be very important.

Bogged in the morass of the moment, I already seemed to have more than I could handle. I didn't know how close Ivey and the Tampa police were to me—and the murderer of Bucks Jordan was no doubt thinking of his own future, not knowing how close *I* was to *him*.

Pressure or action from the Home Office right now might easily mean the *coup de grâce* for me.

I carried the empty beer can to the kitchenette garbage pail. As if the clink of the can were a signal, the phone rang. I returned to the phone, picked it up.

I said hello, and was asked if this was Ed Rivers, and I said that it was.

"You asked me about a couple parties," he said, his voice almost smothered by the sounds of juke box music and laughter in the background. Even so, I recognized the gravelly little voice. It belonged to Gaspar the Great.

"Where are you calling from, Gaspar?"

"Never mind that. A bar. It doesn't matter which one."

"You sound shook, pal."

"No," he denied. Too quickly. "I'm just trying to do you a favor, that's all. If you want those two parties, why don't you try room 212 at the Aeron Hotel?"

"Thanks, Gaspar."

"Ed . . . I'm putting a lot of trust in you."

"They'll never know who told me," I said. "You can depend on that."

"I will. I have to now, don't I?"

"Gaspar . . ." I said his name quickly, but the connection was already broken, leaving me with the question of how he'd known where Kincaid and Smith were located.

Chapter Thirteen

The Aeron was located on the edge of Ybor City, where the narrow streets of Spain yield to the broader thoroughfares of downtown America.

Years ago, before the widespread acceptance of the motel, the Aeron had been a first-class commercial establishment, the sort catering to traveling salesmen and civic club luncheons. Even now it retained a struggling respectability. Cheap, new paper was on the walls of the lobby. There were potted palms, and couches and chairs with slip covers to hide their age.

A few elderly people were clustered at one end of the lobby playing cards and chatting, retired folk for whom inflation had clobbered annuities and pensions that had once promised the inclusion of a few luxuries at the close of life.

I spotted the stairs in the far corner of the lobby next to the old-fashioned iron grille of the elevator. The desk clerk was a comfortably fat old man who took off his glasses now and then to polish them as he read a newspaper.

On the sidewalk outside one of the tall windows that gave on the lobby, I waited until the switchboard demanded the clerk's attention. Then I entered, strolled across the lobby, and used the stairs.

The second floor corridor was long and narrow. A threadbare runner stretched the length of the floor to the red exit light at the further end.

A couple of ancient overhead fans creaked their wide blades sluggishly, stirring the dead, empty heat. I heard no sounds of life as I padded toward the door with the numerals 212.

93

Standing close to the door, I thought of the confines of the car trunk and the agony of smothering in air that no longer held life. The heat seemed to seep into my blood and brains.

I knocked softly with my knuckle. There was no response. Kincaid and Smith were out.

But we could wait—the heat and I, and the gun snugged against my belly and the memory of being buried alive in a car trunk.

The door had a spring lock. I opened it with the steel on my keyring and stepped quickly inside the room.

From across the street, a neon sign spilled a rose haze into the room. I stood against the door, letting my eyes get accustomed to the gloom.

The room was run-of-the-mill. There were two three-quarters beds, a bureau, chest of drawers, writing table. One door opened on a small bath, another to a large closet.

I drew the old-fashioned roller blinds and turned on a small lamp that was on the writing table.

I searched the chest of drawers and bureau quickly. Several of the drawers were empty. Others held socks, handkerchiefs, underwear and shirts. Loose change, an empty cigarette package, and pocket comb with a few missing teeth lay on the bureau where one of them had carelessly emptied his pockets.

Nearly a dozen suits, all of good cut and quality, were in the closet, along with slacks, jackets, changes of shoes.

I went through the garments, coming up with a find composed of tobacco crumbs, book matches, broken toothpicks, and a sheaf of papers from an inner coat pocket.

I carried the papers to the writing table. There were a few blank counter checks from a local bank, a folded, dog-eared story that had been torn from a Spanish language newspaper. I put my foreign vocabulary to work and got the idea the story concerned the execution of a man named Carton. Many months old, the story stated that Cuban authorities had tried Carton for treason to the state and as an enemy of the people. His multimillions of dollars worth of holdings in Cuba had

been expropriated by the state. His widow, with the conniv-
ance of traitors, had escaped Cuba to take refuge in her
native. United States, where a few more million of Carton
money was invested.

The story continued with the usual propaganda blather
about the evils of everything *Yanqui.*

The remaining papers were an Aeron Hotel bill and a small
city map of Tampa.

I went over the story again to see if I could improve my
Spanish. I'd about got the gist of it. I impressed Carton's
name and initials on my mind. R. D. Carton.

I heard the muffled sound of voices in the corridor and
turned off the lamp.

The voices died away. I listened for the deadened fall of
footsteps on the hall runner. Instead, I heard a key touch the
door lock.

I slid the spare .38 from under the waistband of my pants.
With my other hand, I touched the switch on the writing table
lamp.

The door swung open. Kincaid and Smith stepped into the
room, Smith saying he wished he'd stayed in Peru. I intended
for him to wish it a lot more.

I clicked the lamp switch and said, "Welcome home,
crumbs."

Smith's words broke in a dribble of terror as his jutting
eyes spotted me behind the light. Kincaid gasped.

My idea was to disarm them and take them to a quiet spot
for a private, unfriendly chat.

"Close the door," I said.

Kincaid said, "He intends to kill you, Smith!"

With that, Kincaid, already partially protected by Smith's
bulk, shoved the bigger man at me.

I squeezed the trigger as Kincaid dropped behind Smith,
throwing himself toward the doorway. The explosion of the
gun was deafening and blinding in the closeness of the room.

The brain behind Smith's big, pleasant face required time to react. Dumbly, his reflexes accepted Kincaid's words.

I spun toward Smith as his hand came up with a pistol. He was a heavy shadow blocking the doorway.

I pressed the .38 a second time and saw the slug take him in the right side. It jerked his body. A wild, crazy sound came from him. He fired twice in the space of a second.

I heard the slugs slam the wall behind me as I flopped on the floor, rolled behind the bed nearest me for cover.

His third slug gouged through the mattress and breathed close to the back of my head.

"This way!" I heard Kincaid say. "I'll cover you."

I scrambled for the doorway. I glimpsed them clambering out the window in the end of the corridor where the exit light shone, taking the fire escape.

A bullet knocked splinters from the door jamb into my face. I jerked back, breathing hard. Smith had smashed it for me. I wanted out of the room to pick up the pieces.

I wanted it so badly I chanced the open corridor. I ran in a crouch, ready to throw myself flat if Kincaid showed a gun over the window sill.

I knew there was plenty of excitement throughout the hotel. But nobody opened a door or came rushing into that corridor. The impulse of the citizen is to head the other way or dive under the bed when guns begin going off.

Smith and Kincaid were shadows dropping toward the dark alley when I rolled out the window onto the rusty steel fire escape.

There was a flash, a crash in the alley. A bullet scored the brick wall behind me. The darkness made conditions lousy for pistol work.

I held my fire, picking up speed as I took the right-angled turn in the slatted steel stairs.

I stopped for an instant, locating the sound of their running footsteps ahead of me.

A garbage can far down the alley hit the asphalt with a terrific clatter.

Smith screamed, "Kincaid, Kincaid! Wait. . . . I can't go on. . . . I'm hurt. . . . Don't leave me. . . . Damn you, I'll tell if you leave. . . ."

The words were smothered by a single blast of gunfire.

I fired in the direction of the flash, running forward. I glimpsed his shadow round the corner of the building. I was gaining on him. In a little, I'd have him.

Then a spongy mass folded over my feet and ankles. I tripped, pitching headlong. The skin burned off the heel of my left palm as I tried to break my fall.

Shaken and dazed for a second, I managed to roll free of the inert form that had managed in its dying moments to pull itself toward the center of the alley.

There was rancid spilled garbage all about us. I located his head with my hand. There was blood all over the side of Smith's face. Kincaid had killed him rather than risk trying to save him or having him fall wounded into the wrong hands.

Yet in his dying, and quite unintentionally, Smith had continued to serve the brainier man, acting as a block in my path.

I pulled myself to my feet. The sound of Kincaid's quick retreat was gone now. In its place was the rise and fall of sirens.

I ran down the adjacent alley, reached the street that intersected the one on which the Aeron stood. I crossed at the corner and reached my car.

As I pulled off, I saw the arrival of the first patrol car in the rear view mirror.

In my apartment, I felt reaction set in. The inner man twitched and shivered while the outer man with apparent calm shucked his coat, loosened his shirt, and had a long drink of cold water from the refrigerator bottle.

A part of me waited and listened for a knock on the door that would mean Steve Ivey and the Tampa police had connected me with the Aeron shooting.

I had no chance to backtrack and cover. My single choice was to sit tight and hope I hadn't been seen by anyone with a genius for accurate description.

The knock didn't come. But I knew it was a sound in my future. I'd cut too wide a swath this time, passing word in Ybor City that I was looking for Kincaid and Smith. Ivey was bound to get wind of it eventually.

I delegated future trouble to the future. As I managed to unwind a little, a bone-deep tiredness crawled through my nerves and muscles. I took consolation in knowing the pressure wasn't on me alone. I figured I had the ability to crouch down inside my skull and last as long as any of them.

I tried to put myself in Kincaid's skin, behind his eyes. His decision to kill Smith had been swift and absolutely brutal, an action with a very urgent purpose.

I believed I understood the purpose. Carrying my slug, Smith had been too badly wounded to escape. Kincaid had shot him because Kincaid had been afraid to stack Smith's slow intelligence and nerve against the ruthless efficiency of endless police questioning.

So Kincaid's purpose was clear. His drastic measure meant one thing. He couldn't afford to run, not yet. He hadn't finished the job that had brought him to the mainland. He needed more time, right here in Tampa.

I wondered if Kincaid was at this second repeating my own process. Putting himself in my shoes. Trying to figure how I'd got his location. Anxiously guessing how much I knew. Thinking of ways of getting me off his back for good.

I slept that night with the .38 under my pillow.

Chapter Fourteen

The Aeron shooting was front-page stuff the next morning—but down in the lower right-hand corner with a two-column head.

The story said simply that sudden gunfire had shattered the quiet of the hotel. A man identified as Henry Smith had been found dead in the alley, which he had reached via the fire escape. Kincaid had disappeared and was wanted for questioning. Police had not yet established a motive for the shooting.

The remainder of the story consisted of statements by the management and guests of the hotel. Kincaid and Smith had been quiet, respectable-looking tenants, assumed to be businessmen. Guests recounted their terrifying experiences in various ways. One old fellow claimed he'd charged to the second floor when the gun battle broke out, but had been too late to take a hand against the villains.

The scarcity of details in the padded-up story made me feel better. I folded the newspaper and left it for the next counter customer. I paid for my coffee and old-fashioned crullers in the downtown restaurant and went from there to the *Journal* building.

Ed Price, the city editor, was in conference with the managing editor. I sat down in the chair at the end of Ed's desk.

He came across the city room, a sheaf of proofs in his hand, and we traded our usual "Hello, Ed."

He sat down behind his desk. "Do I smell a story?"

"Maybe."

"You're bargaining today," he said.

"Groping."

"At what?"

"I'm not sure yet. If I touch something, you'll get it."

"We should be politicians, Rivers. Okay, we're a couple of back scratchers. I'm willing to scratch first. What's on your mind?"

"R. D. Carton."

Price's thin lips curled in a silent whistle. "You always manage to jolt big, don't you? What's with this Carton bit?"

"You're scratching."

He studied me intently. "You know who he was, what happened to him, don't you?"

"He was rich. He was killed."

"Like numerous others in Cuba's seemingly endless history of such occurrences."

"That was in the papers. I'm more interested in what wasn't in the papers."

"Most of it was there. That continually seething Cuban pot happened to boil over on him. He was found guilty of treason. Whether the charge was valid or not, probably only Carton knew for sure. After his death, his holdings in Cuba were confiscated."

"Was he American?"

"Nope, as Cuban as Garcia or Ochoa. His grandfather was one of the leaders for Cuban independence before the outbreak of the Spanish-American war."

"His widow got away, didn't she?"

Price nodded. "Real story-book escape. Villagers hid her, sneaked her over the mountains at night, finally got her to the coast and aboard a small fishing boat."

"Where'd she land in Florida?"

"Key West."

"Then she came to Tampa?"

"Why, sure," Price said. "Where else?"

"You mean—she's American?"

"Yep."

"And this is her home?"

"Are you kidding?" Price stared at me. "Twenty-five years ago, she was the most beautiful debutante this town has ever seen. When Emily Braddock married R. D. Carton, Cuban and American flags were flying all over the place. Yachts from the two countries remained at anchor in Tampa Bay and stretched the reception into a week-long party."

"Braddock . . ." I said. "Florida cattle."

"And Louisiana oil," Price added. "And she's the end of the string, the last Braddock, the final Carton."

"She never had children?"

Price shook his head. "Considering what finally happened in Cuba, maybe she's had moments of being glad. A teen-age or grown son might have shared a grave with his father."

I stood up. "Where is she living now, Price?"

"On an estate up the bayshore. Old family place. You going to see her?"

"I think so."

"Don't be disappointed."

"Why not?"

"I heard she isn't so pretty nowadays. An old, embittered woman of forty-five." He lighted a cigarette and squinted at me through the cloud of smoke. "My back itches, Ed."

"I won't forget—if I'm able to whittle out a scratcher."

The old Braddock place lay like an immovable slumbering giant surrounded by newer estates in the mere fifty thousand dollar class.

About twenty acres of lawn and an ivy-grown iron fence separated the three story pile of colonial mansion from the boulevard that skirted the bay.

I turned in a sweepingly curved driveway that showed cracks in the concrete. The hedges needed shears like a beatnik needs a barber. There were brown spots in the vast lawn, and bare places where the chinch bugs had feasted unmolested.

The house added a note of gloom to the bright Florida day.

Paint was beginning to curl in spots on the tall, white pillars. A loose flagstone rattled under my foot as I mounted the long veranda.

There were flyspecks of corrosion on the heavy brass door knocker.

The knocker made a booming echo inside, as if the house were vacant in its entirety. I got no immediate response.

Then, from a nearby ground floor window, a woman's brittle voice asked, "What do you want?"

I turned my head. A yellowed lace curtain wafted out of the window, across her face. She brushed the curtain aside.

"I'm not buying anything today," she said. "Didn't you see the no soliciting sign beside the driveway?"

I'd seen a small wooden sign with the letters weathered away. "Are you Mrs. Carton?"

"Yes, but——"

"My name is Rivers. I'm not selling anything, and I don't wish to impose. But it's important that I talk to you. Very important."

She was hesitant. Price had been right about one thing. She wasn't pretty. Her face was fleshless as a mummy's. The cheeks were drawn in. The eyesockets were huge. Her chin was a sharp cut of bone. Stretched over the bony structure was a glaze of skin like yellowed cellophane. Her hair was a dull gray, thinning and dry, pulled to the back of her head and held with pins.

Yet, as she tilted her head to study me, there was a brief hint for a second of a vanished beauty. There was still a certain liveness in her eyes, and the broad mouth hadn't gone completely to bitterness.

"I can't imagine what you wish to see me about, Mr. Rivers. I know of nothing so very important."

"Does the name Kincaid mean anything to you?" I watched for a change in the socket-hidden eyes. If there was a change, I couldn't detect it.

"No," she said. "But if you. . . . Just a moment."

She withdrew her head. The silence of the house returned. Then a bolt snicked on the other side of the door.

The door opened slowly. She stood aside to let me enter.

I took two steps into a vaulted, gloomy hallway where the air smelled of tropical heat and mildew, and the high crystal chandelier gathered dust.

I wanted to walk right out again. Sitting on his haunches, red tongue lolling, was the largest, blackest German shepherd in the western hemisphere. His head was not much larger than a grizzly bear's. He had jaws capable of snapping a bone in two. His tongue dripped as he panted against the heat.

Emily Carton had a grip on the dog's spiked collar. She excused herself and led him to a doorway that opened left off the hallway.

"In, Nino," she commanded.

Even on all fours, the massive dog was taller than her waist. Toenails snicking on the parquet flooring, he obeyed her order. She closed the door behind him.

She stood erectly before me, her body as resilient as bamboo, trimmed down until her dress hung on her in loose folds.

"I see few people these days, Mr. Rivers. When one has been away for a quarter of a century, one returns to few friends."

Obliquely, she'd stated that she had nothing here and nothing remaining behind her. For an instant, her eyes held hatred, for her present status, for the way life had treated her.

"I hope I may be your friend, Mrs. Carton."

"Why? Because I have money?"

"That's a good reason."

"At least you're honest. Who are you, really? Aside from being a Mr. Rivers?"

"A private detective."

"Whatever on earth. . . ." A smile twisted her mouth. "Are you here to frighten me?"

"Not needlessly, I hope."

"I'm not easily frightened," she said quietly. I believed her. Her eyes glinted imperiously as she looked me up and down. I had the feeling that I didn't impress her very much. I glimpsed the past, which was reduced to a ghost inside of her, of that bearing and attitude of a person accustomed to the lifelong privilege of ordering an army of servants around.

"You mentioned the name Kincaid," she said finally.

"Do you know him?"

"Is there any reason I should give you an answer?"

I shrugged. "He's here in Tampa. He seems to have an interest in you."

"Really?"

"He came with another man, named Henry Smith. He was mixed up in a shooting at a local hotel last night. Smith was killed."

"I see." Hands clasped before her, she strolled back and forth a few steps. The vaulted hallway echoed the small sounds made by her flat-heeled sandals. The tomblike house swallowed the sounds as it had swallowed the gay bubbles of laughter and music in another era.

"What makes you think such a man is interested in my whereabouts, Mr. Rivers?"

"For now, I'll just have to tell you that I have my reasons and let it go at that. If you know this man, it might be to your benefit to tell me."

"The police will probably pick him up, if you're thinking he might be dangerous to me."

"Then again, they may not." The closed hallway was sweltering. She didn't seem to notice. I mopped sweat off my face with my handkerchief. "I have ways of finding out things about people, Mrs. Carton. Sometimes it takes time, but I always find out."

Her laugh was the first sign of real animation in her. The idea of intrigue and possible danger seemed to enliven her.

"All right," she said suddenly, "I did once know a man named Kincaid. He was, for a brief period, an overseer on my husband's sugar plantation."

"How brief a period?"

"Oh, I don't know. A few weeks, months. He was a soldier of fortune sort of person. One of those sweaty Americans you find in odd corners of the world. He drifted on."

"Before your husband . . . Before the . . ."

"Before my husband was murdered? You may state the fact in my presence, Mr. Rivers. Yes, it was before that."

"Then Kincaid had no part in what happened to your husband?"

"Gracious, no."

"Or in getting you out of Cuba?"

She shook her head. "No Americans were involved in that. Really, Mr. Rivers. This Kincaid of whom you're speaking may not be the same man at all."

"He's here in Tampa."

"I imagine there are Kincaids everywhere. It's a fairly common name."

"Not Kincaids in Tampa who have kicked around Latin America."

"Why not? Ybor City is full of people who've sought refuge from tribulation in Latin America. You must have a specific reason for believing this particular man is interested in me. Has he said so?"

"Not in so many words."

"Then. . . . ?"

"He was carrying a clipping, a news story in Spanish about your husband's death."

"It must have been months old."

"It was."

"Well!" she said in a sort of gasping sigh. "That's really rather touching, if one is sentimental. Perhaps he is the same Kincaid after all. I didn't know he was that fond of us."

"When was the last time you saw him?"

"When he left the plantation. What happened is obvious, Mr. Rivers. Wherever he was at the time, he was shocked sufficiently by the news of R. D.'s death that he tore the clipping out."

She was lost for a moment in memories. "Yes," she said to herself, "it's nice to know that he was that fond of us. I hope he's in no real trouble, Mr. Rivers."

"That remains to be seen."

"Well, he has no present connection with me. Isn't that what you came to find out? If so, I'll bid you *buenos dias.*"

With that, she went to the door where the horse-sized dog lurked. She opened the door and said, "Here, Nino." She gave me a final nod and smile. "Thank you for coming, Mr. Rivers. If you see Mr. Kincaid, thank him also—for the emotional reaction he found in the clipping. I didn't know he had it in him. I always thought of him as a danger-ous kind of roughneck."

I drove back across the Hillsborough River, which slices Tampa in half, and worried my way through the tangle of downtown traffic to the parking lot near the beatup old office building on Cass Street.

I went up and there was a notice from Western Union hanging on the office doorknob.

I keyed the door open. The outer office held a leather couch and couple of chairs. My desk was in the inner office, along with a steel filing cabinet. The place was stifling. I crossed the inner office and opened the windows. The bustle of Tampa drifted to me.

I sat down at the desk, picked up the phone, and dialed Western Union.

The telegram they'd tried to deliver was from New Orleans. It stated: "Deposit box here registered to Maria Blake. Source says box holder was in town at bank opening this morning. Hope this helps."

I hung up the phone, toyed idly at the cover of the old Underwood, and rocked back in my chair.

Maria Blake Scanlon, it appeared, hadn't been lying. She'd taken my advice and gone to New Orleans. It was my guess she was back by now. There were direct plane flights between Tampa and New Orleans, and a relatively short, quick hop over the Gulf. She'd bounced over, got her jewels, and bounced right back to buy a little more of the relationship that made a travesty of marriage.

I was beginning to pick up the mail that had fallen through the slot in the outer office door, when the wooden box that caught the mail was pulled right out of my hands.

Lieutenant Steve Ivey hadn't come alone. Flanking Ivey as he stood in the now-open doorway was a big cop in uniform.

I said hello and pardon me, and fished the last piece of mail out of the box as if I had nothing else in the world to do.

"Busy, Ed?" Ivey asked, following me inside.

"Nope. Except for the mail." I crossed to the inner office, checked through the half dozen envelopes, found nothing of importance, and dropped them on my desk.

"What's on your mind, Steve?"

"I want to ask you a couple of questions."

"What about?"

"A dwarf."

"Come again?"

"Erstwhile trapeze artist. One time high-liver and free-wheeling spender. Lately down on his luck. Namely—Gaspar the Great."

"What's with him?"

"He's dead," Ivey said. "Got his brains knocked out. Fellow working for the city sanitation department found him about three hours ago. Someone had hidden the undersized corpse for a few hours by dropping it in a thirty-gallon garbage can in an Ybor City alley."

Chapter Fifteen

I went around the desk and sat down. I needed a few seconds.

"I'm sorry to hear that, Steve."

"You knew him, of course?"

"Certainly."

"He isn't pretty now."

"Poor little guy never was."

"You want to come over to headquarters and talk about him?"

"No flies in this office," I said.

"This is official, Ed."

"Okay." I stood up. "What are we waiting for?"

We went downstairs and got in a cruiser that was parked at the curb. We drew the usual curious glances from passersby.

The uniformed cop acted as chauffeur. Ivey got in the back seat with me, taking off his floppy panama hat and mopping his peeled-egg pate. He looked like somebody's uncle, with or without the hat.

We rode the few blocks to headquarters, and I walked with Ivey to his office.

He got a drink at the water cooler in the corner of the office and hung the hat on a nearby hook.

"Have a chair," he said, going behind his desk.

He waited until I'd seated myself in the heavy wooden chair at the end of the desk.

"Ed, what's going on amongst the little people in this

town, the midget and dwarf citizens who colonized here in the days of the carnies?"

"I don't know what you mean," I said.

"I think you do. Tina La Flor tried to contact you. She disappeared. Gaspar the Great called you from a bar last night. It's the last trace we have of him alive. He's found dead several hours later. You get our point of view?"

"Sure. You want some answers, and I don't blame you."

He studied me for a moment. I met his gaze blandly. I was feeling differently inside. It had been no great trick, with Gaspar the Great dead, to trace his movements and find that he'd called me. I wondered if Ivey planned next to hit me with the connection between Gaspar's tip to me and the Aeron shooting. A corpse named Smith and one named Gaspar were isolated items in the files, bearing no relationship—unless Ivey knew why Gaspar had called me. Then the implication would jump right out of the files and slap him in the face.

I never like to get loose with the truth when talking with a cop. But I was prepared for Ivey's next question.

"What was on Gaspar's mind, Ed?"

"Tina La Flor," I said. "He wanted to know if I'd turned up any trace of her."

"Why did he think you might have?"

I shrugged. "I did a few steps of legwork after you came to my place."

"And did you turn up her whereabouts?"

"No," I said. "I'd have called you. I told Gaspar I wasn't on the case, that my interest had been personal. I suggested that you'd be a better source."

"You asked him what his interest was, I'm sure."

I nodded. "He said Tina was an old friend. He didn't give me any more than that."

"Then he hung up and that's the last you heard from him?"

"Yes."

"Ed," he said coldly. "You're a liar."

"Have I ever lied to you before?"

"No. I've always considered you a sort of unofficial adjunct to this department."

"Let's keep that status very much quo," I suggested.

"I hope we can. I've a feeling that something big and dark is going on in your end of town, and you're in it up to your neck." His eyes pinched at the corners. "So deeply in it that you've lied to me about Gaspar and Tina as well. I don't want to see you get hurt, Ed. I'd hate to be the one to hurt you."

"You'd do it thoroughly."

"As thoroughly as possible," he said. "I'm no whiz of a detective, but as long as I'm in this office I intend to work at my trade. You'd better think more than twice, Ed, before you flounder into the undertow."

I was glad he didn't know the grip the undertow had on me already.

I stood up. "I'm free to go?"

"You know you are," he said, his face reddening with anger. "How long could I hold you with what I've got?"

"Long enough for me to call a lawyer."

"Get out of here!"

I got out, quickly and quietly.

With Ivey a closed door away from me, I wandered into the squad room. There, I picked up additional details on the murder of the dwarf Gaspar.

It appeared that the little fellow had been killed in his hotel room by a person he knew. Nothing in the room had been disturbed. A smudge of blood had been found on the window sill. His lifeless body had been pushed out the window into the alley below. The murderer had taken the fire escape out of the hotel. In the alley, the afterthought of an idea had struck him, and he'd shoved the lifeless, misshapen body into a nearby garbage can. The murder had taken place in the early hours of morning.

Doing an unobtrusive fadeout from headquarters, I caught a cab to the lot where my car was parked. Motionless exposure to the Florida sun had heated the interior until the seat and steering wheel were blistering to the touch. Movement of turgid air through the open windows helped a little as I got the heap rolling and moved with traffic into Ybor City.

My mind moved faster than the tires sucking at scorched pavement. I was certain of the linkage between the murders of Bucks Jordan and Gaspar the Great. Kincaid and Smith were the bond between the two. They'd been after Bucks, and after Gaspar's tip to me about the location of the pair, the dwarf had been killed.

It seemed reasonable to assume that both had been permanently put away because they were dangerous to a person, or persons. The delay in killing Gaspar simply meant that he hadn't been regarded as a danger right away, not until my appearance had shook him up a lot worse than I'd known.

I wondered if he'd sent me to the Aeron on the gamble that I'd get killed facing both Kincaid and Smith.

With Bucks Jordan's death ever-present in his mind and my survival of the shooting scrape, Gaspar had run out of nerve. And out of life.

And he could have told me many things. . . .

I found a parking place on the narrow street and wedged the car in. The sidewalk ahead was massed with a gay crowd that gave bursts of applause for the guitar-laden trio in the window of a department store who played lively songs and told livelier stories in Spanish.

I crossed the street and entered a narrow restaurant. A beautiful girl with olive skin and hair blacker than black was at the cash register.

"Is Rafael in?"

"To you, *si*. Señor Batione is in back."

I thanked her and soaked up the air conditioning as I

moved past the tables to the door in the left rear of the place. The door opened on a short corridor which dead-ended in another door.

I knocked on the dead-end and the door opened noise-lessly. A second girl, sister to the one in front, glanced over her shoulder and spoke to the interior of the office. "It is Ed Rivers."

She must have received a nod, for she stood aside grace-fully for me to enter.

Both the girls were daughters of the massive, sleepy look-ing man reclining on a white leather couch that filled the far wall of the luxurious office.

His smiled showed gold-filled teeth. He raised his short-fingered, fat hand in greeting.

"*Qué tal?*"

"Fair to middling," I said.

His daughter turned a deep leather chair slightly so that I could face her father.

"Cigar, Señor Rivers, or a drink?"

I shook my head and thanked her. With a graceful turn of her body, she crossed the office, seated herself at a desk, and resumed typing on a large, electric machine.

I eased into the chair the girl had offered. Rafael Batione sighed. "The heat, it bothers you as it does me, Ed." There was a lot of him to bother, about three hundred and fifty pounds. In cotton slacks and short-sleeved shirt, he lay as if he never intended to move from the air conditioning. "But it is not the heat of the climate that brings you here."

"An occurrence in Cuba," I said.

"I see."

I listened for a moment to the clatter of the typewriter a world away from Batione's seeming indolence. Miami is the publicized window on Latin America. There are a few men in Ybor City who are more than content to keep it that way, who worked to keep attention on the window. Rafael Batione was one of those men.

"You know the R. D. Carton case?" I asked.

He began to sit up slowly, spilling his feet to the thick carpet, pushing with his hands. His eyes, buried in masses of soft flesh, centered on my face.

"You know that his widow is here," I went on. "And you must know also that there is in Tampa Bay a schooner called the *Sprite* with a Peruvian registry."

"Is there a connection, Ed?"

"That's what I want to find out. Something disappeared off that boat. It triggered the deaths of two men."

The mention of death failed to make the slightest break in the rhythm of the distant sounding typewriter.

"I come to you," I said, "because I'm beginning to wonder what scheme is being hatched."

"There is none, in Ybor City. If there is a scheme, it was not hatched here. What do you think was taken from the boat?"

"I'm not at all sure, now. I'd thought it might be papers, a plan."

"This was not the destination for any such thing, Ed." He stood up. In that position, he lost the soft, sloppy look. He took on the appearance of a wrestler capable of clubbing an opponent senseless with the heel of his hand. "You have my word," he said quietly.

"And I accept it. *Gracias.*"

"We do not deal in murder, Ed. Our concern is for the homeless refugee, the helpless *peon* who chops cane or digs in the mines twelve hours a day for twenty cents, the child carrying a gun in a dictator's state militia."

"Mistakes can be made," I suggested.

"Not in our business," he said.

Chapter Sixteen

I blistered my rump on the car seat and my feet
on the pavements during the remainder of the afternoon trying to get a lead on Tina. It had begun with her. If not the
sole key, she'd jangled plenty on the keyring. I didn't want
her ending up in the manner of Gaspar the Great. I had to
have those points of information she'd held out on me. She
owed me at least that much.

By late afternoon, I was still up the creek and I'd run out
of paddles. If anyone had told me a little doll with such
unique physical characteristics would vanish without trace
in Ybor City, I wouldn't have believed it.

With a tired pumping in my feet and a dismal ache in my
head, I dragged up the stairs to my apartment.

I dunked in a cold tub while I cooled the mucuous mem-
branes with beer. I was plagued with the feeling that I should
know where she was. Something right under my nose should
tell me.

Common sense told me she was probably at the bottom of
Tampa Bay with a big chunk of metal tied to her. But when
you gumshoe your way through enough years, cases and
people, you develop a subconscious ability to add up things
that have escaped conscious notice. The result now and then
is an annoying mental dislocation that most cops call a
hunch.

In a change to fresh clothes, I went in the kitchenette, put
a Cuban sandwich together, and got cartons of slaw and
potato salad out of the refrigerator.

I slid a plate onto the table and started to spoon slaw
out of the carton. I stopped with the spoon halfway between

carton and plate. I stood there looking at the plate while juice from the slaw dripped from the shredded mass on the spoon.

The subconscious worm crawled right out of the cocoon and spread its wings. A breath of relief jolted out of me.

The plate, plus a chance remark, told me where Tina La Flor was hiding. There was little chance of her leaving before I arrived.

I sat down and ate my dinner.

A breeze came and died, ushering in a night in which the dead heat was a vacuum, as if a squall were building up in the Gulf. The night needed a lashing by a swift rain to make it livable. I suspected the rain would fail to reach the mainland.

I parked the car half a block away from the Cardezas house. I crossed the street, walking quickly, and mounted the sagging front porch. Across the street a gang of kids were playing tag, shrilling Spanish annoyances at the little boy who was "It."

I heard the muffled rise of mood music and sharp crackle of six-guns from the Cardezas TV set.

I knocked. Mrs. Cardezas answered, her comfortably ample body filling the doorway. In addition to the TV glow, a small lamp was lighted in the living room behind her.

She thrust her round, full face forward to look at me, the room light etching the coils of her shiny black hair.

"Well . . . Señor Rivers. Have you word of Tina?"

"Yes," I said.

I brushed past her into the room. Her voice rose in an exclamation of surprise and irritation. "Señor Rivers, until you are invited . . ."

"Save it," I said.

Little Miguel was belly down on the floor, watching the TV with his elbows propped on the floor, his chin propped on his hands.

He squirmed around to look at me. A little girl slid out of a chair and started for the doorway. I crossed the living room after her. She wore tattered sneakers and a faded print dress. Her hair was in pigtails.

The boom of my footsteps caused the speed of her exit to increase. She darted toward the rear of the house.

With four or five long steps, I was reaching for her. Mrs. Cardezas threw herself in front of me.

"Señor Rivers! What is the meaning of this? You cannot break into my house . . ."

"Please, lady," I said.

She grabbed my arms. She was a big woman and a strong one. Little Miguel came up and started kicking my shins, darting in and out, giving vent to his enjoyment in excited Spanish.

Mrs. Cardezas' weight banged me against the wall. Miguel got in an extra good one on my right shin. I howled softly in pain.

A little girl with black hair and olive skin—not the one I was after—came rushing into the room from the back part of the house.

"Mama! . . . Mama! . . ."

"Rosita," Mrs. Cardezas gasped, sweating to hang on to me, "run next door. Get Señor Figuero and scream for many neighbors. Tell them a madman has broken into our house!"

I began to get sore, and fear jolted through me. I know how those Latin neighbors would react on such a hot night.

The little figure I was after—Tina La Flor, of course—had reached the kitchen.

Mrs. Cardezas was draped around my neck, her heavy strong arms locked together, her weight pulling me down. I reached back to break her grip without hurting her.

Little Miguel made like a billy-goat, lowered his head, and charged. I saw him out of the corner of my eye. Mrs. Cardezas' shifting weight reeled me to one side. Miguel missed his target, cracked his head against the wall, sat on the floor, and started wailing.

Sweating in desperation, I firmed my grip on the heavy, smothering arms. Mrs. Cardezas cried out as I tore myself free of her.

I heard the kitchen door slam. I charged the sound, banged my way outside, and tripped off the low back steps.

I skidded to a stop on hands and knees, looking up in time to see the small, running shadow in the darkness. I scrambled after her. Just as she reached the corner of the house, I grabbed the collar of her dress.

"Lemme go, you big lummox!" She squirmed around fighting, kicking and scratching.

In the front yard Rosita was yelling frenziedly for assistance for her ma-ma. A man's voice answered her, and a second man's voice answered him. A couple of women joined in.

Tina gave a good account of herself, but I smothered her attack without breaking any of her bones.

Holding both her hands behind her back with one of mine, I gave her a hard shake.

"Now you listen to me, you little witch! You've caused me more trouble than half the hoods in Tampa. I'm fed up to here, see? You simmer down, but quick, or I'll turn you over my knee and blister you good before I throw you to the cops."

She became still. "Okay, Ed," she said bleakly. "I know when I'm licked."

To insure against her doing any more broken field running, I tucked her in the crook of my right arm, her legs and arms dangling.

I fore-armed sweat off my face while I considered what to do. I heard more neighbors gather from various points of the compass in the Cardezas front yard. The din rose in volume.

They shouted wild instructions to each other. I realized the steadier ones were fanning out, coming around each side of the house.

I ran across the backyard and took the low rear steps into the kitchen. I closed the door, threw the bolt latch, and propped a can-bottomed chair under the doorknob.

Mrs. Cardezas, charging toward the rear of the house, almost collided with me. She drew up, seeing that I had Tina and had re-entered the house.

"You go out there," I told her, "and restore the peace of the evening. Tell them it's all right."

Mrs. Cardezas hesitated.

Tina gasped, "Do as he says, Mama Cardezas . . . Ed, I can't get my breath in this position and all the blood is running to my head. Would you mind not killing me for the moment?"

Mrs. Cardezas went outside. I heard her voice rising over the babble of her neighbors.

I parked Tina on the edge of the kitchen table in a sitting position.

She felt her stomach gingerly where my arm had circled. "How'd you find me?"

"The other evening I called a Tampa cop, Gonzales by name, to ask about a man named Jack Scanlon. I also asked Gonzales about you. He said they had no lead on you, that it was as if you'd grown up beyond recognition.

"Later, in the light of the plates, it occurred to me that maybe you hadn't grown up—but down. Into childhood, so to speak. Just another kid in a houseful of kids."

"What's this about plates?"

"The first time I came here Mrs. Cardezas was setting the table for dinner. Six plates. But only four kids and herself. Five people. It finally dawned on me to ask myself who was the sixth person, the fifth kid. There were no other grownups around."

"I guess it doesn't take much to tell you a whole lot, Ed," she said rather dismally.

"Sometimes a wall has to practically fall on me. It wasn't

very nice of you to be hiding right here among Mrs. Cardezas' brood while I've had my naked neck stuck away out."

"Maybe not, but what else was I to do? For your sake I had to stay away from the cops."

"Big hearted you," I said.

"Don't sound so bitter, Ed. You know it's the truth. If I'd told them about me and Bucks, and you trying to help me, they'd have stuck you under the jail. You—you didn't kill Bucks, did you?"

"Would it matter to you if I had?"

"Yes," she said. "A million times I've regretted dragging you into it."

"Well, with that much decency to start with, we'll see how well you can level now," I told her.

Mrs. Cardezas came into the kitchen. The furor in the yard had died down.

The big woman glanced from me to Tina. "It's all right, Mama Cardezas," Tina said.

Mrs. Cardezas continued to look at the tiny woman with tenderness. Then Mrs. Cardezas turned her head toward me. "Señor Rivers, we did what Tina asked. . . . For you personally there is no ill feeling."

"Now that's downright kindly of you, m'am," I said. The edge on my words caused her to redden.

"Ed's pretty much put out," Tina said, "and I think you had better just go quietly into the other room, Mama Cardezas."

"If you need me . . ."

"She will send you a telegram," I said.

With backward glances over her shoulder, Mrs. Cardezas started out of the kitchen. Little Miguel's head showed, thrust past the door jamb. Tear streaks were still on his cheeks, but he was recovered well enough to eye my shins hungrily.

"And take him with you," I suggested.

When they had gone to the front of the house, I turned to

Tina. She sat making pleats in the front of her dress, not raising her eyes to meet mine.

"Ed," her whisper faltered, "I have some money . . . I'll pay you for . . ."

"Money wouldn't hire me to go through what I have, Tina. I've been slugged, shot at, stuffed in a car trunk and left to die."

I realized she was crying. It was for real. She was trying hard not to. "What can I do now, Ed? Go to the police?"

"Are you kidding? I'm one-half of a lucky jump ahead of them right now. What you said about Bucks Jordan's death in relation to me still goes, only more so. It was me involved in the Aeron Hotel shooting. I'm the nudge that caused Gaspar the Great to lose his nerve, suddenly become dangerous to somebody, and get himself killed. If the cops were briefed and moved on me right now, I'd be lucky merely to lose my license and spend the next twenty years or so in Florida state pen. There's nothing I can do but see it to a finish."

"I'll help all I can, Ed."

"While you're helping, you bear in mind that if you tell me one more lie I'll break your lovely little neck."

"What do you want to know?"

"The obvious. When you came to me that night, Bucks Jordan wasn't after you *per se,* was he?"

"No."

"He was after an object, an item."

"Yes."

"It came off the schooner *Sprite,* didn't it?"

"Yes, Ed," she said meekly.

"What was it?"

"A half million dollars."

Chapter Seventeen

I wasn't too surprised. I'd known it was big. "A half million," I said, "in what?"

"What do you mean, in what?"

"Jewels? Bonds?"

"Plain old American cash, Ed. Five hundred one-thousand dollar bills not much larger in a tight package than a couple of pocket-sized books."

"Whose money was it?"

She stared at the floor and said bleakly, "Bucks said it was anybody's. Up for grabs. Belonged to anyone who got it and kept it."

"You know better than that, Tina. That kind of money always belongs to someone."

"Sure," she said as if she hated herself. "Bucks was telling me what I wanted to hear, roping me into the deal. He was making it easy for me to rationalize and kid myself. He said the money was part of a crooked deal and we had as much right to it as the next person."

"Did he know what the deal was?"

"He had an idea. He came aboard the *Sprite* once without D. D. hearing him. She staggered out of the cabin, blind drunk, and made a crack to her father before she realized Bucks was there. If the liquor held out, she said, she'd remain a happy assassin until it was over. Alex Lessard told her to shut up. Then he tried to pass off the remark as drunken talk. But Bucks got the idea they were planning to kill somebody."

"With Jack Scanlon," I said, "as the imported trigger man."

"I wouldn't know about that, Ed."

"It fits him like his skin. Did Bucks know the identity of the target?"

Her pigtails swished about her slender neck as Tina shook her head. "No. He didn't know about the money, either, at that time. Later he and Scanlon were drinking in a waterfront bar. Scanlon got in a boastful mood. He made a slip about the money."

"I still can't figure you in," I said. "Why didn't Bucks take the money himself? Why a partner and a split of the take?"

"The money was in a package, inside Alex Lessard's own stateroom. The cabin was never unlocked, even when he was inside asleep. The only way to slip into the cabin was from outside."

"Outside?"

"The water," Tina said. "From the water."

I glommed onto the idea. "Through the porthole."

"Yes. Lessard left it open in this climate for obvious reasons. No one would have viewed it as a hazard. For a normal-sized person to get through it was out of the question. I nearly broke my shoulders when Bucks helped me in, small as I am."

"He took you out by boat?"

Tina nodded. "He had a small, lightweight plywood boat stashed in a mangrove stand not far from the bait camp out there. He eased us out, not taking the oars from the water as we neared the *Sprite*."

She was stilled for a moment as she remembered the quiet, the darkness, the rasp of water against the hull of the schooner riding at anchor.

She drew a thin breath. "When we got out there, we heard their voices. The Scanlons and Lessards. They were up on the foredeck, drinking and making idle chit-chat.

"Bucks gripped the rim of the porthole and steadied the plywood rowboat. I was wearing tight jeans and a slip-over knitted shirt, no shoes. With his free hand, he latched onto my belt and helped me inside the cabin.

"We didn't have any trouble—at first. I'd brought a small flashlight with me, one of those the size and shape of a cigarette lighter. I found the package under Lessard's bunk. Before I left the cabin, I tore a corner and made sure the package contained money.

"Bucks helped me out of the cabin and we headed for shore. Then suddenly, I heard Jack Scanlon call out, 'Lessard! Bucks Jordan's prowling around out there.'

"There was a moment of absolute silence on the schooner. Lessard yelled, 'Jordan, is that you? What are you doing?'

"Bucks hissed at me not to say a word. Believe me, Ed, I wasn't about to. I was crouched on the bottom of that plywood job by that time.

"Next, I heard D. D. say, 'You'd better check the cabin!' Footsteps, Lessard's I guess, ran across the deck of the *Sprite*. A few minutes after that, we heard them scrambling into one of the schooner's small boats. We were a good distance off by then, the sounds drifting to us over the water.

"Bucks was rowing like crazy. One of them in the other boat had a powerful flashlight. I thought our gooses right then were parboiled, baked and fried.

"We reached the mangroves before the light caught us. We plowed our way in, not minding snakes or anything else. I was shaking like I had pneumonia.

"We hid there while they searched. Scanlon came so close one time I thought he was going to step on me. Finally they decided our head start had given us a chance to get out. They moved in other directions, still searching, and Bucks and I had the chance to get out.

"He was scared silly, the chicken in him really spreading its wings. He wanted the money then and there, but I had it stuck under my shirt. I was afraid he'd take off without me. So I told him I'd yell if he tried anything funny.

"I couldn't keep up with him, and he didn't want to hang back. He kept hissing at me to come on, come on.

"He reached the old asphalt road where the car was parked ahead of me. One of them, Lessard or Scanlon, had come out of the mangrove a hundred yards away. He'd seen the parked car's shadow in the heavy flashlight beam.

"He pot-shotted at Bucks, and all Bucks wanted was to get out of there. He scratched off."

"Leave you?" I asked.

"He'd have left his own mother to a cut-throat pirate crew at that moment, Ed." Her lips twisted in her pale face. "Scanlon and Lessard legged it to the bait camp to get a car. I started walking. When I reached a main thoroughfare, I had my first bit of luck for the evening. A taxi stopped, about the third one I yelled at. It was empty, after taking a fare up the bayshore.

"I went home, bathed, changed clothes, had a drink to try and drown the shakes, and then Bucks showed up. We opened the package . . . That's when he really blew his stack and yelled double-cross."

A short, bitter laugh came from her. "We got about twenty-four hundred dollars for our trouble. The outside bills were thousands, all right, but the rest were singles, little peanut one-dollar bills.

"The way he was storming, I saw he was past the point of reason. I knew he'd stop making verbal threats any minute and start trying to use physical violence to get at what he thought was the truth.

"I ducked in the kitchen and out the back door. He stumbled around in the darkness mouthing that he would find me and break my neck.

"My car, the one with the special brake gadget, was parked in the driveway. He struck matches, looking inside of it. When his widening search carried him across the yard, I slipped in the car.

"He heard the car start and almost reached it before I got out of the driveway. When I rounded a corner, I saw his headlights coming after me. I was out of my mind with fear, afraid of the police, the people on that boat, Bucks. Bucks was the most immediate fear."

"So you came to my place," I said.

"I had to have help," she said miserably, "or thought I did. Now I wish. .ʻ. . But I just didn't have the nerve to let Bucks get hold of me.

"I thought I'd given him the slip a few blocks back. I parked my car in the far end of the parking shed at your building.

"Bucks spotted me going in. I heard him coming up·after me. That wicker table was in the hallway . . . Your transom was open . . ." Her voice filtered to nothing.

"When you left my place," I said, "you took your car and came here?"

"Yes . . . The car's down the street, closed in a neighbor's garage. The night we went to the *Sprite* Bucks used a rented car. Ed . . . I haven't been very brave in any of this."

"No, I guess you haven't, Tina. Have you made any plans?"

"Plans?" Her laugh was brittle, her green eyes far too bright. "I've cowered here and hoped blindly . . . that you'd come out okay . . . that you'd work it out."

As she looked at me, her face grayed a shade further. She was past the point of tears now. Her lips were blood-less and wrinkled. Her face seemed to collapse at the edges and grow wizened, the face of a tired, old woman, a woman so old that living had become a mere memory.

"Ed . . ." My name was a strangled sound on her lips. "I don't expect you to excuse me. I don't blame you for hating me. But if you understood . . . just a little . . . if you were inside of me, looking at the world from everybody else's navel. . . .

"When I was a kid, I used to wonder what was so terrible about me that even my parents didn't want me. I outgrew that, to an extent. But I was tired, Ed, of being a person wrapped in a package this size. I was tired of the people staring and making cracks, tired of earning a living by being a freak.

"When Bucks came and told me about all the money, I didn't want to listen. But he knew how I felt. He'd been in carny life. He sensed the feelings of a freak.

"I didn't care about the money, Ed. I wanted what the money represented in freedom and independence. Instead of coming in the stage door, I wanted to sit out front with enough money to command a respect and attention I'd never had."

"You had those things, Tina, with a lot of people."

"Yes—I know. I know now. With the people who counted, the Ed Riverses, the Cardezas, the waiters and the boys in the bands where I worked. But it was the others who counted too much, Ed. The boors and wise-crackers. Now . . . what now, Ed?"

"You'll stay here, under wraps, until I have a chance to square myself," I said.

"You trust me not to take a powder?"

"Got any place else to go?"

"You know I haven't. They'll spot me in an hour if I get in the open."

"Then it seems to be safe to trust you," I said. "Later, you're slated for the police."

"I know. I'll keep the appointment."

At the kitchen door, I paused. Her contrition was genuine. She sat woebegone, forlorn.

"Go wash your face," I said, and my voice was rough, because I was, after all, supposed to be mean-mad at her.

I spared myself any further possible experiences with Mama Cardezas and little Miguel by stepping out the back door and going around the house.

The neighborhood was quiet except for the usual. Kids playing in the hot darkness, hide-and-seek by this time. A girl's laughter as a boy courted her on a ramshackle front porch across the street. A trio of amateur calypso singers down the block singing the tale of a banana loader who got a tarantula on him.

I got in my car. The whirring of the starter cut into the final portion of the song.

I turned at the next corner, heading for the bayshore without learning if the poor guy died of tarantula bite before his true love arrived with a final kiss.

I hit the downtown traffic lights perfectly and made good time, crossing the river and wheeling up the bay with the dead jellyfish taint of the tide-flats filtering into the car.

I left the car on a side street a quarter of a mile from the Carton estate. Walking rapidly, I turned in the driveway and kept to shadows as I neared the gloomy hulk of house.

One room in the place seemed to be lighted, downstairs, front corner. The stand of once-beautiful pines off the driveway towered now over a field of thickets and palmetto. I prowled the field until I found what I was looking for, a stout pine knurl about as long as my arm. Lying on the ground where it had blown from a tree, it had seasoned out. The resin, baking out, had given the club a stony hardness.

I freed the club from its nest in a tangle of briars, hefted it in my right hand.

I moved to the driveway and pitched a handful of pine bark against the side of the house. The place remained silent, that single light glowing behind old lace curtains that billowed gently in the open window.

I squatted and searched with my fingers until I found a broken piece of concrete at the edge of the drive. I tossed the missile into the untrimmed shrubs that drooped beneath the lighted window.

This time there was reaction from the house.

I knew Mrs. Carton had opened the front door when I heard the sharp question from the veranda. "Who's there!"

I threw a chunk of pine bark into the thicket at my left.

"Nino!" Emily Carton commanded in a suddenly crisp, savage voice. "Out there . . . Get him, Nino!"

Chapter Eighteen

I placed my back against a pine trunk and backhanded sweat from my eyes.

I saw the leaping shadow of the dog leave the veranda. His toenails fell like spilled tacks on the driveway.

I let a hissing breath past my lips. He came quickly. I caught the glint of his eyes and teeth as the enormous dog bunched his muscles and sprang, a sound lower than a mere growl in his throat.

I had the urge to break and put the tree between me and the brute. Instead, I brought the club around.

The nearly petrified pine knurl met him straight on the schnoz. Better than three hundred pounds of the combined weight of dog and man were behind the impact.

Nino did a half somersault, crashing on his side in a thicket. Threshing, he gave a roar that would have done credit to a lion. He was really mad, as dangerous as a lion, if he got out of the thicket.

I heard no votes for giving him a second chance. I went in fast, while he was floundering. I swung the club and missed him.

The next time, I didn't.

The pine knot popped him on top of the great, black head. He fell, shuddering. The shudder quickly passed, and he was as quiet as a new-born puppy after his first big dinner.

The big dog's breathing rasped. I hadn't wanted to kill him, hadn't meant to. I was glad he was still alive. He wasn't responsible for the job he'd been trained to do.

I heard the front door of the house slam shut. I plowed through the brush growing under the lighted window. The screen was old, rotten and I ripped it away.

I threw my leg over the sill, parting the wafting curtains. Emily Carton had grabbed the telephone on a nearby table. She was dialing frantically.

She threw a glance at me, dropped the phone, and ran for the door at the far end of the room.

I caught her as she was yanking the door open. With my fingers on her elbow, I swung her back. She stumbled, kept her footing, and came up short about ten feet away.

The eyes were blazing in the shriveled, skull-like face. Her thin, wiry body shook with rage.

"How dare you!" she screamed. "You insufferable . . ."

"I'm not going to hurt you, Mrs. Carton."

"You'll get out of here if you know what's good for you! You're forgetting that I'm Emily Braddock Carton! I'll have you . . ."

"Shut up!" I said.

She did. Not because she was particularly afraid of me. She was dismayed at what she interpreted as my effrontery.

"I have never been treated . . ." she began.

"You were treated a lot worse in Cuba," I said.

She gave me a stare. "I shall call the police, this instant."

"Go ahead," I said. "It might be best for all parties concerned. Might stop an assassination."

She cooled visibly. She seemed to be listening, but the big dog was still out cold.

"What do you mean, Mr. Rivers?" Her breathing slowed. She was getting her anger under control.

"I'm not completely sure," I admitted, "but I'm getting the picture."

She turned slowly, as if looking for a place to sit down. The room was a long living room, furnished with heavy stuff that had been real luxury thirty years ago. Now the needlepoint and brocade were as faded as the curtains. The baby-grand piano, once white, had yellowed with age. The whole room had a feeling of rats' nests snuggled in the corners.

"What picture is that, Mr. Rivers?" she asked with faint disdain.

"Your husband's silhouette is in one corner," I said. "Down about midway, a boat called the *Sprite* has been sketched in. There are several dollar marks scattered around."

"Sounds like a most surrealistic painting."

"That's right. You never know what you're going to see next—or the meaning of it."

"Assuming there is a meaning."

"Any time half a million dollars is involved, you'll find a meaning, Mrs. Carton."

"Half a million?"

"Of your money, Mrs. Carton."

"Ridiculous!"

"You deny that you're financing a plan to kill a man in Cuba—to have him killed as your husband was killed? You have nothing left in life, except the hunger for revenge. You're a very rich woman, able to do something about it."

"But I deny what you say."

"Then you're in grave danger yourself."

"Equally ridiculous."

I shook my head. "The schooner came here with a purpose. The Lessards, Scanlons, Kincaid and Smith were all a part of that purpose. If you're not planning to put the finger on some-one in Cuba, then we have to conclude that the hand which struck your husband down is reaching for you."

"Really? Why?"

I shrugged. "The murderers, the expropriators always fear retaliation. They never feel safe. They are of the blood-purge school."

"What are you trying to do, Mr. Rivers? Frighten me into hiring you?"

"No," I said. "I'm sorry for you, as I'd be sorry for any woman driven half mad by the complete wreckage of her life. Disaster is especially difficult for a queen. But I'm not here for hire, just answers."

"Too bad I haven't got them."

Beyond her, the lace curtains ballooned. I felt a breeze across my cheeks. I saw the change in her eyes as she looked past me.

I turned on eggshells, because I knew that's the way I'd better turn.

Kincaid was standing in the doorway that gave to an adjoining room. His eyes were puffy, his shirt rumpled as if he'd been taking a nap. He'd opened the door noiselessly and entered without putting his shoes on.

He stood with a lithe looseness of body, the sharp angles and planes of his face without expression. His expression was reserved for the eyes under the high forehead. The gun in his right hand was centered on my middle.

"I'm very tired of you, Rivers," he said slowly. His gaze moved past me. "How'd he get in, Mrs. Carton? Where is the dog?"

"Immobilized."

"Rivers has a habit of immobilizing his enemies. But he's all through with that now," Kincaid promised.

"I was on the point of calling for you," Emily Carton said, "when I realized he was coming through the window. I was afraid you wouldn't be at your best, fogged with sleep, if I revealed you were here. I grabbed the phone to make Rivers think I was alone. I was certain our voices or ensuing commotion would awaken you."

"Very clear thinking," Kincaid said.

I had to agree. It was no wonder she'd managed an escape from Cuba with the world falling in on her. She was intelligent, capable, accustomed to command.

"What do I do with Rivers, Mrs. Carton?"

"We can't have him found here. Take him to the Scanlon cottage. I'll call you there. We shan't be needing the cottage much longer."

"We're going ahead?"

"Yes."

"Half a million is a fortune, Mrs. Carton."

Her eyes burned at the thought of the loss. "Don't remind me, Kincaid! We can't take any further risks trying to recover the money. We'll have to accept the loss."

"We, Mrs. Carton? When I got in touch and braced you with the idea, the deal was . . ."

"I know what the deal was, Kincaid! I have another half million—and another—and another." She was almost screaming at him. "Does that satisfy you?"

"Sure, Mrs. Carton. Business is business. If you keep details clear as you go along, there can't be any misunderstanding."

"We won't have a misunderstanding," Emily Carton told him, "so long as you do precisely as I say."

"Okay, Mrs. Carton. Your word is good enough for me." He motioned with the revolver. "How about we move out, Rivers? I'm sure Mrs. Carton has looked at your kisser long enough. Mrs. Carton, please take his gun. Then get my shoes." She lifted my gun, tossed it on a chair.

She fetched his shoes and jacket from the next room. He slid his feet into the shoes without taking his eyes off me. She kneeled and tied the laces.

He slipped a flashlight from his jacket pocket when we were outside.

"To the left, Rivers. The back of the house."

A black sedan of a low-priced make was parked behind the house out of sight.

"You in front," he said.

As I slid under the wheel, he eased into the back seat. I felt the muzzle of the revolver touch the back of my neck.

"Take the bay road, and don't break any traffic laws."

As we rolled along with stars looking at themselves in the vast sweep of bay water, the revolver eased from my neck. But I knew it was there. And how quickly Kincaid would strike.

"Too bad you went to all that trouble, Rivers, and ended up without the half million bucks."

"You think that was my motive?"

"What else?"

"How can you be sure I haven't got the money?"

"Don't try to string me," he said. "If you'd found the money, you'd have stopped sticking your nose in."

"There's a lot you don't know."

"Not interested. If Mrs. Carton's willing to write off the loss, so am I. Before dawn we'll be at sea. We won't care what happens on the mainland after that."

He was saying that they'd have no fears from the mainland. I was the only person with the tip-off, the truth about the *Sprite's* mission, for the authorities. Kincaid intended to see that the truth wasn't told.

"Who is the man?" I asked.

"Man?"

"In Cuba."

"Oh, there are a lot of head cheeses in Cuba, Rivers. There are big head cheeses and smaller head cheeses. The fellow we're interested in is pretty much a chief head cheese. He got that way largely through what he did to R. D. Carton. Carton had trusted that guy with his life, too. Can you blame Mrs. Carton for feeling the way she does?"

I approached the turn-off, slowed at Kincaid's bidding, and drove past the bait camp on the pot-holed asphalt road.

The outlines of the Scanlon cottage swam into the edges of the headlight beams.

As I braked the car in the corner of the sandy yard, Jack Scanlon came around the far side of the house. In the full glare of the headlights, he was sweaty, disheveled. His face had lost its lazy look. His black hair was lank, plastered to his forehead and temples with sweat.

"Who's there?" he called, a touch of panic in his voice.

"Kincaid. Watch it. I've got Rivers in the front seat."

Scanlon ran to the side of the car.

Kincaid said, "What's the matter with you?"

"It's Maria. She's off there in a thicket. She won't come out."

"Well, go in and get her. A psycho wife is your problem."

"I've tried. I can't catch her."

"We've too many other things to think about," Kincaid said, his voice low and savage. "What's she doing hiding like that?"

"We had a fight."

"What about?"

"I'm going to leave the stinking cow," Scanlon said. "I can't stand her any longer."

"You're going to get her out of there," Kincaid told him. "That's what you're going to do."

"Listen, you can't make me stay with . . ."

"I'm telling you, Scanlon."

"And I'm telling you," Scanlon said. "This whole idea has blown up."

"No, it hasn't."

"Like hell. And I'm out, see? Count me out. The money's gone. We can't find it, and things have been getting hotter with every passing hour."

"And your feet have been getting colder. But there's money. Plenty of money."

Scanlon looked at Kincaid's shadow in the back seat. "What do you mean?"

"Mrs. Carton is taking the loss. Now you get your wife under control and head for the *Sprite*."

Scanlon stood in an awkward position, forearm half-raised

to his sweaty forehead. He turned jerkily, cupped his hands about his mouth. "Maria," he said in a louder than normal voice, "I didn't mean it."

She didn't answer.

"Maria . . . honest . . . I wasn't myself. I didn't mean those things . . . my nerves. . . . They're on edge from the pressure of the past few days."

A rustling sound came from the thicket beyond the front yard.

"Please, Maria . . . I'm sorry . . . I'll make it up to you, darling . . ."

Because she wanted so very much to believe, she believed.

She came slowly out of the thicket. Blocky, bovine, her drab hair stringing about her face, she came slinking forward. She was on her feet, of course, but she had the attitude of a person crawling on the belly.

"Jack . . . I couldn't stand it without you."

"I know, hon. I'm sorry."

"When you threw those jewels back in my lap, I thought I'd lost you for good."

"What jewels?" Kincaid muttered quickly.

With a bare turn of his head in the direction of the car, Scanlon said, "She had some jewels in a safe deposit box in New Orleans. She hopped over and back." To Maria, he said: "I was just shook up, baby, from the waiting and all. You'll never lose me."

She held out her arms then and rushed forward. Scanlon, with a distaste she missed, put his arm about her shoulders.

"Okay," Kincaid said. "Get moving."

"How about Rivers?"

"I'm going to kill him," Kincaid said.

Maria Scanlon started. Jack tightened his grip on her shoulder.

"Don't you think about it, Maria," Scanlon said. "Kincaid knows what he's doing."

A brief desire to help me showed in her eyes. But she yielded to the pressure of her husband's arm, and they moved away in the night.

Chapter Nineteen

Kincaid waited. It seemed to me an incredible amount of time passed. I heard the slow, hard coursing of blood through my head. I felt as if a fog of steam were smothering me. The steam did nothing for the dried-out stiffness of my mouth and throat.

The gun stayed inches from the back of my head.

"All right," Kincaid said, satisfied at last with the utter silence of the night. "Get out."

I got out. A brief trembling passed through my knees.

"There's a marshy place beyond the yard, Rivers. It will do. They'll be a long time finding you."

He motioned with the gun for me to turn around. "Keep your hands shoulder high. Now move."

I walked down the long beam of light from the car with the eerie feeling that my feet weren't touching the ground.

We reached the brush, a stand of tough, young pines. The light came through in patches. Plenty for him to cut me down if I tried to run.

A pine bough, heavy with needles, raked across my face. I barely felt it.

The second bough made an impression on me.

I let my right hand lock about the next limb. It was tough as a willow whip. I threw myself forward and down, releasing the pine bough.

Kincaid was right behind me. My motion held his attention. I heard him start to speak my name like a curse. Then the pine bough slashed him across the eyes.

I pinwheeled and went in under the bough. He was off-

138

balance, clawing at his eyes. My shoulder hit him in the gut. My hand locked on his gun wrist.

With a shrill gasp of pain, he went over backward, his leg crumpled under him. I swarmed him, giving him no chance to recover.

I hit him three times in the face so fast that my fist made almost a continuous sound.

He tried to wriggle free, kicking, striking at me blindly. The gun slipped out of his hand. We threshed, clawing at the gun. I was unable to get a clean punch. I butted him under the chin. His head snapped back, and I felt the starch go out of him.

I rolled free, grabbed him by the collar as he tried to flounder to his feet. I hit him twice dead on the chin. His knees knocked together. When I released his collar, he fell face forward in the sand.

Finding the gun quickly, I thrust it under my belt. With his collar again in my grip, the back of the collar this time, I dragged Kincaid out of the brush and across the yard.

Inside the cottage, I let him slump in the middle of the living room. I turned on lights as I searched the place. In the kitchen I found what I was looking for, a coil of strong clothesline.

Kincaid's loose, unconscious form offered no resistance as I trussed him up, hands behind him, legs drawn backward and connected to his bound wrists by a doubled length of line.

I dragged him to a bedroom closet and shoved him inside. I wasn't careful about bruising him. But it was comparatively cordial treatment. As a prison, the closet was nothing like a car trunk.

Although not listed in Scanlon's name, there was a phone in the cottage. I left it off the hook, preferring Mrs. Carton to get a busy signal rather than the endless ringing of an unanswered phone.

No clean towels were in the kitchen or bath. I used my

handkerchief to clean the worst of the grit from Kincaid's gun. Then I turned off the lights and left the cottage.

In Kincaid's sedan, I rolled into the parking area of the bait camp. Cutting the lights, I got out of the car and walked to the edge of the water.

Fiddler crabs scurried across the sand, seeking their holes. No tide was running, the bay lapping softly against the pilings of the pier and the rental boats in their slips.

The twin masts of the *Sprite* stood straight and steady against the night sky. In addition to the red points of her navigation lights, the schooner showed a haze of white light on the foredeck.

I waded into the water beside the bait camp pier, moving gingerly to keep from splashing. When the water was waist deep, I took the gun in my hand and held it above the water level.

I checked each flat-bottom as I passed it. In the fifth or sixth, I found a pair of kapok life preserver cushions.

Pushing the bouyant cushions ahead of me, I waded on until the water was neck deep. Then I stacked the cushions, rested my upper chest on them, and continued moving toward the schooner with a silent scissor kick.

As the long minutes passed, I began tiring more from the effort and strain of remaining silent and unobserved than from the physical exertion. I moved with my gun hand resting on the upper edge of the kapok, out of the water, my legs driving without breaking the surface.

Finally, I heard the mumble of their voices, crescendoing now and then in angry peaks of sound. Scanlon was telling Lessard that he was up-to-here with the deal. He was pulling out. Lessard was none too happy.

"I depended on you, Jack," he said bitterly.

"But everything has changed," Maria put in, "and it's not the same bargain that Jack entered."

"That's right," Scanlon said.

"Let's all have a little drinkee," D. D. piped in.

Alex Lessard paced the foredeck. "Damn it," he cried in acute frustration, "why does it always have to turn out so rough for me? Everything I touch . . ."

"You're a hard luck guy," Scanlon said. "Some people are that way."

"The old lady is going to be sore," D. D. said.

"I can't help that," Scanlon said. "I'm going to tell her."

"We'll tell her together, Jack," Maria said.

"Oh, shut up!" he told her, his voice heavy with contempt and disgust.

I moved under the shadow of the *Sprite's* hull, inching my way toward the ladder. I grasped it, held on. The kapok cushions drifted away.

In the water, I was buoyant. I knew my weight would cause a slight list of the hull when I started up the ladder. I drew in a breath, got set, and went up, fast.

As my head and shoulders cleared the edge of the deck, I snapped the gun toward them.

"Hold it, Scanlon! The rest of you—stand nice and easy."

Scanlon's hand stopped before it dipped in his rear pocket. They stood unmoving, staring at me as I climbed on deck and stood with water puddling at my feet.

Then D. D. broke the paralysis with a drunken, senseless giggle. Alex Lessard shot her a dark look.

"Too bad he didn't fall for our hopeful little lies and away with me to Jacksonville, ay, Papa?" she said to Lessard.

Drawn so tight inwardly he was shaking from it, Lessard said to Scanlon. "You told us Kincaid had taken care of Rivers."

"That's what Kincaid said," Scanlon stood white-lipped.

"Ed," D. D. said, "do you mind if I have a little drinkee?"

"D. D. . . . !" Lessard said through the swollen veins in his neck.

"Oh, you fool," she said quietly. "You miserable, doomed-to-failure fool. Can't you see it's all over?"

"Not yet," Lessard said. "Not yet!"

"You never know when to stop banging your head against the wall, do you, father dear? Well, I do. I'm thirsty. I'd like to stay blotto the rest of my life. But since Rivers is too big and real to wish out of existence, I'm going to do the next best thing, for myself. Ed, I'm not guilty of a thing beyond conspiracy and coming along for the ride. You need a state's witness?"

"That's right," Scanlon said.

"Bitch!" Maria screamed. "Disloyal bitch!"

"Go die, cow. You'd be better off. Your brain's as putrid as the rest of you. You stink. I know it. Your husband knows it. You know it yourself."

"Knock it off," I said. "I do mind about that drink, D. D. You just ease up behind Scanlon and lift the gun from his back pocket."

She sighed, then did as she was told, holding the gun carefully away from her where I could see it.

"That's the ticket," I said. "Now drop the gun over the side."

D. D. was the usual supple vision in skimpy shorts and halter. Lessard was wearing his faded khaki swimming trunks and nothing else. Neither had much chance of concealing a deadly weapon in what they were wearing.

As D. D. carried it to the rail and opened her fingers, the gun ker-chugged in the water.

"Now," I told her, "frisk Maria."

D. D. moved behind Maria. Her hands patted Maria's sweaty, rumpled cotton dress.

White-lipped, Maria said, "When we left you with Kincaid, I pitied you, Rivers. I wished for a way to make it easier for you. Now I wish Kincaid had killed you."

I let it pass.

"No cannon or atom bombs," D. D. hiccupped. "About that drink. . . . I've earned it, pal."

She weaved to a small deck table and picked up a glass and bottle.

Lessard edged forward a couple of steps. "Rivers, you're not a totally unreasonable man."

"Meaning?"

"I've never met a man yet who didn't have his price."

"Maybe you've always been in the wrong company."

"Surely there must be a way we can come to terms."

"There is," I said.

"You do have a price, then?"

"In this instance—yes."

"Good. Name it."

"A murderer," I said.

Chapter Twenty

"That's great, Ed," D. D. said over the rim of her glass. "Real great. The killing's to be in Cuba . . . in the future."

Lessard opened and closed his hands and looked as if he wished his daughter's neck were between them. "Shut up, D. D.!"

"She hasn't told me anything I don't already know," I said. "Maybe *the* murder hasn't taken place yet—but a pair of others have already, here in Tampa. Bucks Jordan and a dwarf named Gaspar the Great. I wish I'd never heard of either of them. I wish you people had never crossed my path. But we don't always get our wishes, do we?"

"You think one of us killed the both of them?" Maria asked.

"Isn't she a dumb cow, Ed?" D. D. giggled. "Why else would you be out here?"

"Do you know which one of us?" Maria persisted.

"Yes," I said.

"How much more do you know?" D. D. inquired. As her father started to speak, she shushed him with a gesture. "No, papa darling. I want to hear. I want to know how a man like Rivers operates."

"I know most all of it," I said. "A few of the minor details are obvious assumptions from the larger facts.

"Emily Carton's life was wrecked by her husband's death. Things that had been important in the past became meaningless. money, social position, even personal grooming.

"I'm sure that Kincaid, learning of Carton's execution and

144

knowing the widow's temperament, sought her out and showed her the possibility for revenge—at a price.

"She took a new grip on life, a warped and evil grip. Her money was again useful—for an unholy purchase. She would put up whatever amount was necessary, a half million dollars, if it would bring death to the man in Cuba responsible for the execution of her husband.

"The next scene takes place between a couple of Caribbean vagabonds. Kincaid and you, Lessard. I don't imagine you were strangers to each other."

"Real pals," D. D. said. "They once ran some cocaine out of Brazil."

Lessard seemed not to hear her this time.

"Kincaid has got himself a guy to do his dirty work, Henry Smith. But Henry doesn't exactly qualify for an assassination. Lessard knows a man who does, a man who barely missed a firing squad after a Latin American revolt."

"Sounds like you're talking about me," Scanlon said.

"No kidding! How much did they promise you, Scanlon? Ten thousand? Fifteen, maybe?"

"You're telling the tale," Scanlon said.

"Simple enough, too. Emily Carton had Cuban contacts. They helped her flee the island. They'd assist with this. The *Sprite* would put into a cove at night. You'd go ashore, Scanlon, and meet the Cuban contacts. They'd help you in and out. In to kill the man Emily Carton was after, out when the job was finished.

"Everything was going beautifully—and then the double-cross. The money disappeared, a cool half-million dollars Emily Carton had put up to finance the expedition."

"Bucks Jordan," D. D. said, "took the money, darling."

"That's what you think."

"He took it and passed it on to someone else," D. D. said with alcoholic persistence.

"That's the way it was supposed to appear."

"Really? I'll bet he passed it on to you, after all. You

convinced Kincaid and Smith he hadn't, but I'll bet you were being terribly clever."

"D. D.," Lessard said heavily, "*will* you shut!"

"Certainly I won't, father. I believe Ed is a rich man and has come out to finish us all off for his own safety."

"My safety doesn't lie in finishing you off," I said, "but in nailing down a murderer.

"You've thought Bucks Jordan passed the money to someone else who killed him because he could identify that person. Perfectly logical, on the face of it. Bucks was killed at the first opportune moment to make you think exactly that, to make it appear absolutely certain that he had stolen the money and become the victim of a double-cross.

"After Kincaid and Smith decided I hadn't received the money, the search continued for an unknown person, someone known only to Bucks. Still logical.

"Your efforts to find this shadowy stranger, this unknown, have failed because there has never been any such person. Bucks failed to get the money. He never had his hands on it.

"Sure, he came after it with a midget named Tina La Flor. He slid her through the porthole of your cabin, Alex. She got out with a package. She thought she had the money. The only thing she had was a ringer.

"Someone else had already gained entry to the cabin in the same manner, using a dwarf named Gaspar the Great. Later, this person had to kill Gaspar when the dwarf saw the pressure building, showed signs of breaking, and became a danger."

The silence of the sea came over us for a short moment.

Maria Scanlon said almost gently, "A double murderer . . ."

"Yes," I said, "and we know, don't we, Maria?"

"I—" Her hand raised to her throat. Involuntarily, she moved closer to Scanlon. She looked at him and swayed. He caught her arms above the elbows, his face dark with revulsion, distaste for her.

"I . . . don't feel very well," she faltered.

"I'm sure you don't," I said. "knowing how you feel about him. But he's never wanted you, Maria, only what he could get from you. Now he doesn't need that. He can throw your remaining wealth, your jewels, back in your face. He's got plenty, a cool half-million dollars. Of course, it cost him about twenty-four hundred. He had to make up a dummy package to keep the theft from being known. The ringer that Bucks and Tina took from Lessard's cabin—after Scanlon and Gaspar had lifted the real package and left the dummy."

Lessard took a step toward the larger man. "Scanlon—you!"

"Don't pay any attention to Rivers," Scanlon said. "Can't you see he's lying to save his own skin?"

"Get a load of laughing boy," I said. "I'm guilty—so I come out here, stick my neck out, tell a lie I can't back up."

"Let's hear you do some backing," Lessard said, his voice a quivering cork against the eruption inside of him.

"Okay," I said. "It shapes up simply enough. Scanlon cares for nothing or nobody. He recognizes no ties in any bargain. He got to thinking about that money and the risk he was going to take for a small piece of it.

"He wanted the money, all of it, and none of the risk of a Cuban killing. But how? If the money simply disappeared from your cabin, Lessard, the rest of you would immediately recognize an inside job. He'd never get away from you. He knew he was dealing with people who'd hound him to the ends of the earth to get that money back.

"There seemed one safe and certain way for him to do it. He must definitely make it appear that an outsider had stolen the money. Then the outsider must die, apparently killed by a second, unknown outsider. You'd run yourselves ragged. He'd string it along until the delay and pressure gave him an excuse to back out of the whole Cuban deal. He'd take his leave of you, give Maria the boot, hie himself to climates unknown, and live like a king the rest of his life."

"There's several of us," Scanlon said, gripping Maria's arms tightly. "Are we going to stand here and listen . . ."

"We are," Lessard said. "What led you to this belief, Rivers?"

"First, it was Scanlon who tipped Bucks about the existence of the money. They were together in a bar and Scanlon was supposedly loose-tongued from liquor. If I had the whole of that conversation, I'd probably find that Scanlon hinted how the theft might be pulled. The midget population of Tampa is sizable, and Bucks knew a lot of them in his carny days. The market for midgets isn't what it used to be. A lot of them are down on their luck and Bucks had a strong lure to corrupt one of the little people.

"Scanlon's big mistake was in his too-ready identification of Bucks the night Bucks and Tina stole the dummy package. They were in a light plywood boat, some distance away on the water. You, Lessard, saw them too indistinctly to make a sure identification. Even *after* Scanlon called Bucks by name, you said, 'Jordan, is that you?'

"Scanlon knew who was out there because he'd intended for Bucks to be there. He'd been waiting and listening, one night, two nights, maybe more, for Bucks to steal the dummy.

"With the fact clearly established in your minds that Bucks had stolen the fortune, Scanlon waited for a chance to get rid of Bucks and set you off on a red-herring chase after an unknown person. Scanlon's chance came after Bucks and I had a fight in Tina's cottage. Scanlon simply walked in and clobbered Bucks Jordan's brains with his own blackjack.

"The killing of Gaspar served a double purpose for Scanlon. It got rid of a danger. It saved whatever money Scanlon had promised the dwarf.

"Talking with Gaspar in Gaspar's room, Scanlon saw growing fear in the little man. If Gaspar cracked, he realized, he'd have more than the police to worry about. You'd tumble to the fact that *two* little people were connected with the theft of the half-million. Scanlon knew that you then might reason that Bucks had been a fall guy, for a schemer in your own ranks."

Lessard said in a choked whisper, "Now what, Rivers?"

"Now I want proof," I said. "Kincaid is locked in the Scanlon cottage. He values his neck. So do you, Lessard. The only way out for you is to help me get the proof I need on Scanlon."

Scanlon threw her straight at me, the wife he'd vowed to love, honor and cherish. Not caring how many bullets she took, so long as it gave him a break, a chance.

I tried to dodge Maria. My wet feet slipped on the deck.

Scanlon kicked at me. I pitched back, trying to raise the gun. I didn't want to kill him. That job was for the State of Florida. But I had to slow him down.

I fired from a slumped position. A sudden movement by him caused the slug to catch him in the body, lower and further in than I'd intended.

He grabbed his stomach, pitching to one side under the impact. He accepted the change of direction the bullet had given him. He went over the side, hitting the water in a crazily pinwheeling dive.

Maria Scanlon's hands were tearing at me. "He's ill!" she shrieked. "Can't you understand him? He needs help—not pecking from all the other chicks in the brood!"

I back-handed her hard to get her away from me. I looked at the dark water, trying to spot Scanlon's lighter shadow.

I heard D. D. say, "Well, how do you like it now, father dear? I say to hell with it. To hell with everything!"

Lessard was close beside me, peering over the rail, paying no attention to his daughter.

He was mumbling under his breath, "I'll get him. I'll make him tell where the money is . . . I'll get him. . . . The rat . . . the dirty, double-crossing. . . ."

Maria put an exclamation mark on his words by slamming him across the side of the head with a heavy crockery pitcher the Lessards used as a cocktail mixer.

Lessard slumped, out cold. I raised my arm, warded off

Maria's next blow. I grabbed the pitcher and jerked it out of her hand.

She tried to strike me with her fists, and I shoved her hard across the deck. She was brought up against the side of the cabin.

I heard Scanlon swimming then, and I saw the pale blur of him making for shore.

I hit the water in a belly-busting resemblance to a dive.

I heard Maria give a cry and come crashing in the water behind me.

Later, I discovered that she'd never learned to swim well. All her life, she'd been too painfully aware of what she looked like in a bathing suit to have much to do with the water . . . later—when she failed to reach shore alive.

Right then, I was putting everything I had into trying to catch Scanlon. Like a sheep dog, I swim long but not fast.

Then I realized I was gradually overtaking him.

I neared him, Reached for him.

I grabbed him, by the ankle.

He kicked at me feebly and threw a few weak punches at me when I swarmed him and we went under.

He slipped free of me for a moment. Then with salt water boiling in my nose and ears, I touched him.

He had a final surge of strength in him. It carried him a few yards ahead.

As I broke the surface, I saw him looking back at me. I struck out after him again.

When I reached him this time, I knew I had him. The bullet he'd taken had drained the strength from him. The water around him caught starlight and the glow of the *Sprite's* deck lamp, and the reflection held a hint of red.

"Scanlon," I gasped, blowing water out of my nose, "you're dying."

"No," he said, "I won't die. I can't die. It wouldn't be right."

"Because of the money?"

"I'll live . . . to spend the money. . . ."

"No," I said, "tell me where the money is. I want proof, Scanlon. I have to have proof."

"You . . . go . . . to the devil, Rivers. . . . If it hadn't been for you . . ." Salty water gagged him. He tried to rear up. He fell forward, the water closing over him.

I was blind with hatred for him for a second. Then I knew I couldn't leave him to the prowling barracuda and blood-scenting sharks.

I grasped his collar, half-turned on my back, and got his head wedged against my chest out of the water.

The bay and I fought for the possession of Scanlon. I managed to thresh the remaining yards until there was bottom under my feet.

I dragged him on shore. Then I fell on hands and knees beside him.

The pounding lessened in my head and I looked at him. A faint groan came from him. He was still alive.

I straddled him to pump some of the water out of him. My fingers came in contact with his waist. They went rigid, so rigid they hurt. He'd taken no chances. He was wearing it on him, around his waist in a flat money belt.

Proof.

Half-million dollars worth of beautiful proof. . . .

The leathery bait-camp proprietor was standing on his screened front porch when I staggered to the cottage.

"What's going on out there?" he asked. "I thought I heard a shot."

"You did. The guy who took it may make the grade if we get an ambulance quick enough. I used his shirt for a compress to slow the bleeding. Now I need your phone."

"Phone?" he said blankly.

"For police business."

"Police? Oh, sure." He jerked the door open and gestured toward the phone. It was on a wicker table in the screened porch area where the proprietor did most of his living.

I picked up the phone and got an ambulance started out

for Scanlon. Then I called Lieutenant Steve Ivey at his home number. I identified myself and said, "Get this, Steve, and get it quick. Call the Coast Guard and pin down the schooner *Sprite*. She's here legally, but as part of a plan to put her to illegal use. She's Peruvian registry and the CG will know where she's anchored. Then shoot a squad car to her residence and pick up Mrs. Emily Braddock Carton on suspicion of conspiracy. Next . . ."

"Emily Braddock Carton!" he shouted. "What's going on?"

"You were right when you said I was into something up to my neck, Steve. Now—just trust me. Briefly. You won't be sorry. I got a few people for you to put through the wringer, a couple murders you can clear off the record, a mess of bloody details you'll want to mop up."

The tone of my voice got to him. "Where are you, Ed?"

I gave him the location of the bait camp.

"I'll be right out," he said.

"Cordon off the area, and bring plenty of help."

"I intend to—and you'd better have explanations ready."

"I'm loaded with them," I told him.

I hung up, and remembered my promise to Ed Price of the *Journal*. I tried his home, his favorite bar, his office. He was working late.

"If your back itches," I said, "join Steve Ivey. He's on his way to see me."

"Thanks, Rivers. I'm on my way."

I swung the wet, flat money belt, enjoying the slap of it against my leg. "It's a long story," I said. "It began with a beautiful little doll who stands three feet tall." I thought about it for a moment; then I said, "Unhappily, she had an ache inside of her to be as big as she imagined the rest of us. . . ."

Printed in the United States
By Bookmasters